The Travelling Man and Other Stories

A "Griot African Storytellers Competition" Anthology

Theme: ADVENTURE

Authors

Kalu Rejoice Chioma, Radha Zutshi Opubor, Wilmah
Kudakwashe Mupa, Favour Modekwe, Ifeyinwa Ogwo,
Brian Ochieng, Melinda Barthel, Tanyi Nkongho, Khutso
Modika Eron, Ivan S Mooh Mooh

Editor: Dr. Quinta

Published in the United States of America by Squinti Publishing, Washington DC.

SquintiBooks.com

Cover illustration by Thamba Tabvuma

Hardback ISBN: 978-1-947350-05-2
Paperback ISBN: 978-1-947350-06-9
eBook ISBN: 978-1-947350-07-6

DEDICATION

This book is dedicated to all those who dare to dream

ACKNOWLEDGEMENTS

Special thanks to Vivian Agbegha and Dr. Helen Nwanosike for their many contributions to the success of this project

PREFACE

These stories are the top 10 entries from the Griot African Storytellers Competition (contest.squintibooks.com) which was set up to encourage unpublished authors from all over Africa to hone their craft.

The theme for the 2020 competition was "Adventure." The stories presented here represent the entries that adhered to the theme the best, as well as told compelling stories.

We hope you enjoy reading the stories as much as we enjoyed curating them.

CONTENTS

Ogbanelu (The Valley)

By Kalu Rejoice Chioma

A story from Nigeria

It's a different year!

I am a Nigerian girl of the Igbo tribe. *Not your regular Igbo girl.*

I was born and bred in the western part of the country; I like to think of myself as a Yoruba girl by association. As such, I had never been to my village. I didn't know how to speak my native language; matter of fact, I knew next to nothing about my culture.

My grandparents would always rant about the failure of my

parents to raise me up with cultural awareness whenever they called. They would whine on and on about how they yearned to see me and how much of a mind sore it was that their only grandchild had never been to the village.

"I cho ka anyi nwo ka ma anya fun ya na anya." Do you want us to die before we see her? They would always ask.

I knew this phrase because of its rampancy. Sometimes I felt sorry for them; I really wanted to see them too. I begged my parents every year to take me to the village, but my pleadings were always rebutted with excuses: they were busy, there was no money for the expenses, they had other obligations to fulfill and many other ones of similar flimsiness. *So it seemed.*

That's why this year is different.

For the first time, my ears received the news they had been itching for at this time of the year. *December.* We were travelling to the village! In that moment, I could have worshipped my parents. I think I did because I was beyond elated. My clothes were always packed at this time of the year in anticipation of a miracle but I had given up this year so I didn't pack them. No wonder they say you get answers to your prayers when you least expect them. Nonetheless, it would be the first time I would be packing with joy.

It was travel day!

I had heard travel stories from my friends who visited their villages regularly. I know the feeling of being a listener who could only grasp by imagination. It was different this time; I was experiencing everything I had imagined. The fast-moving trees as the momentum of the car increased, the long roads that seemed to always end at a point because that was the farthest my eyes could see, the hawkers diligently clamoring for sales, the bumpy roads in *Ore* and the sweetly smooth ones in *Benin*. I would sleep for hours and would still wake up on an endless road. I loved the view, but I was tired too.

"How long before we get there mummy?" I asked my tired-faced mum.

"Very long," she replied with pouted lips.

"Urgghh," I replied drifting back to sleep.

The River Niger!

I had heard so much about this landmark. I had been taught about it too, but for the first time, I was seeing it.

We were just about to enter *Onitsha* from *Asaba*. My mum's excited violent shake woke me up.

"Don't you want to see the famous River Niger?" she asked in reply to my sleepy grumble. Like a white board wiper on marker, her question wiped the sleep of my eyes and replaced them with awe.

"Wooooowww!!" that was the most my brain could come up with in that instance.

Drift.

"You really need to see the River Niger! It's the biggest River in West Africa! I couldn't believe my eyes when I saw it, wow! It so sad you don't travel, press harder, beg your parents *now*."

I really thought Uchechi was just trying to get to me and rub her fun in my face, so I replied with a smug face, but after seeing the river, I wanted to apologize as it was so beautiful!

"Stop! Come down now!"

The angry-faced robber shouted at us with his gun pointed at my dad.

"Please leave my daddy alone!" I was wailing by now. Scary occurrences never go well with me, so I was thankful when a gentle shove woke me up. *Oh, it was a dream.*

Except that it wasn't, the same voice ordered my dad to come down, only this time the voice belonged to a police officer.

"What happened, mummy?" I asked, still scared.

"Nothing your dad can't handle" she replied, but she was obviously pissed.

It was already dark but I couldn't tell what time it was. They were saying something about vehicle documents. My sleepy gaze followed my dad's hands as he brought out his documents from the car's glove compartment and handed them to the angry-faced policeman who didn't seem satisfied. The look on my dad's face showed he was losing his patience and I watched him slip a thousand naira note into the man's hands. His face immediately looked pacified. I registered mentally to interrogate my dad on his act. He had always told me bribery was corrupt, but right now I just wanted to sleep.

Drift.

"*Nne mooooooo.*" My mother!

"*Hewu!, Lekwa nu nwam oo.*" Look at my child!

The excited adulations of a familiar voice brought me back to the present. I opened my eyes, still in the back seat of the car. Her head was leaning in with the widest smile revealing lipton tea-stained teeth. The car light was turned on so I could see her oval eyes, just like my mum's. She had tied a Ghana scarf on her head and an *Ankara wrapper* around her waist. *My grandmother.* Her arms were wrapped around me before I even realized they were stretched out waiting to be embraced. *So warm and motherly.*

The next day, it felt like the whole village came to welcome my parents. It wasn't surprising given how long it had been since they last visited, but I was the one bearing the brunt. Everybody wanted to touch me, greet me, grin at me from ear to ear and, most annoying of all, they spoke to me in our dialect to test my knowledge of the language. I was irritated because it was obvious that I didn't understand what they were saying and when they had their fill of the ridicule, they switched to English while giving ten thousand reasons why it was sad that I could not speak my language and calling out my parents for not raising me with cultural awareness. The excitement of the visit started to wane.

The next day, Uncle Ugo, my mum's favorite cousin came over with his kids. Unlike me, they were accustomed to village visits, they had all the cultural awareness I lacked and knew the nooks and crannies of the village even with their eyes closed. It was almost intimidating to be the novice and I wasn't getting along well with everything. I just wanted out.

Amaka.

"That's my name. I'm thirteen years old and my dad tells me we are second-cousins!" She heartily explained.

It was the third day after our arrival, as usual villagers were still pouring in from all parts of the village, cheering on in the spirit of the season. Uncle Ugo visited with his two daughters. They seemed to contrast in all observable ways. Amaka was light-skinned, tall enough for a girl of her age and cheerful in a breezy way. Onyiyechi who was a year younger had a caramel-toned complexion, was shorter in a wider ratio, and reserved. She sat at a spot for most of their visiting time just watching everyone walk and talk. She seemed bored to me, I could relate to that and that endeared her to me, but I didn't bother starting a conversation.

"Would you like to take a stroll?" Amaka continued.

My default response would have been "no", but I realized I hadn't given the slightest attention to her introduction earlier and I didn't want to come off as rude, so I said,

"Sure, if you'd show me around."

I was really grateful that someone finally wasn't testing my language comprehension skills for fun, so we would get along fine.

"Ok, let's go then," she replied.

It became a routine, going out with Amaka in the afternoon and returning in the evening. My olfactory lobes were getting used to the musky smell of *Afara* village, my eyes to the beautiful trees, my legs to the moist earth and deep caves. Countless times I would peep into the old huts of the older folks and shout *"Nde wo nu oo,"* *I greet you,* like I had been saying it from birth. Amaka had taught me a few words, especially the popular greetings, that significantly reduced my noviceship and I became enthusiastic to learn more.

"Do you know about *Ogbanelu*?" she asked as we walked home briskly.

"You know I don't, ha!" I said with a sheepish laugh.

"Just giving benefit of the doubt" she replied.

"But I want to know, so tell me," I said.

"Ogbanelu is a valley in the eastern side of the village, a very deep one. It has a big river flowing through it, with sand steps that lead down into the valley. It's said to be the most dangerous to go to because of how deep it is. The valley itself is enclosed by trees. I went there with my dad last year but I only had an outer view because he did not let us down the sand steps. But the little I saw was so beautiful!" she explained dreamily.

"Sounds interesting. Will you go again this year?" I asked hopefully.

"I want to. I asked my dad but he said he won't be taking us there this year for whatever reason. I know the way there, I just need company. Would you like to come?" she asked.

"Hmm...yes, but don't you think we should ask our parents?" I have never been one to go against my parents.

"I have a better idea. Just tell your mum you're going to Ogbanelu with us, that way you won't be going without her permission" she suggested.

"*With us*? Who is 'us'? I asked with suspicion.

"Let me teach you something, when you don't want your parents to inquire too much, just add '*them*' to the name of any known family member. It is presumed that you're going with the family. In this case, just say you are going to Ogbanelu with Amaka *them*," she explained.

"Is that a thing or what?" It sounded funny to me.

"It's a norm" she said laughing.

"It doesn't change the fact that I'd be lying. It's just you and me, not "*them*," I replied.

"No, it's not. Onyiyechi is coming with us," she replied, a glint of mischief in her eyes.

"Really? Amaka, be serious." The thought of Onyiyechi coming along piqued my interest. I always felt guilty stealing her sister away, while she stayed back. Something about her intrigued me. It was like she was in a dark place.

"It might interest you to know that it was her idea," Amaka replied.

"No way!" I exclaimed.

"We leave at noon," she replied with finality.

Noon.

True to Amaka's word, Onyiyechi came along. It felt like it was someone else in her body. The aura around her was different. She talked and she even laughed. It looked like she had grown two inches taller but that was because her shoulders were not slouched as usual. No straight face today.

"I never knew you could talk," I said to her as we walked through the tiny road path leading to Ogbanelu.

"Now you know" she replied, almost coldly.

"There's just something different about you today," I pressed on.

"I love adventures," she replied dismissively. I decided I'd let it pass.

We had gotten to the foot of the valley and *ohhhh*. Amaka's description was definitely deficient but that was no fault of hers because I wouldn't have done better myself. A thick mass of green surrounded the valley, and there was a beautiful entwinement of trees I couldn't identify. The mushy smell was almost intoxicating and one could hear the movement of the water from the foot of the valley. On tiptoes, I could see the picturesque chain of rounded hills and wild flowers giving a view of green- and yellow-tinged nature.

Southward lay the sand-steps Amaka had talked about. Two young ladies who were just coming up with their gourds of water muttered some greetings our way. This was quite unusual because older folks always waited for younger ones to greet them, but they didn't seem to care. I wondered why they didn't ask for our parents since everybody in the village was caringly nosy, but I figured they were in a hurry.

Someone was talking behind me. It was Onyiyechi. I couldn't hear the words but she was muttering to the trees. Weird.

"Let's go in!" Amaka's voice invaded my thoughts.

We walked steadily down the sand steps for fear that they would give way. My heart was racing and something didn't seem right to me but I wasn't about to be the odd one again.

Amaka seemed so at ease. Onyiyechi was obviously lost in everything. The more I looked at her, the more my intuition signaled red. For the first time, they looked like twins. I saw more resemblance as I looked from one to the other, and they wore matching outfits. *Why hadn't I noticed that earlier?*

I walked up to Amaka, while Onyiyechi was just some feet ahead of us, conversing with nothingness.

"You know, when she was younger, she would fall sick and start crying to be brought here. We never understood her connection with this place but she got better every time. It was really hard on everyone when we moved to the city. That's why I brought her along, we could always tell our parents that she really wanted to come here so we accompanied her," she explained.

"You mean you're using your sister?" I was irritated.

"No, I'm not. She does want to be here. I'm just helping her and we don't have to tell anyone if we are not asked. We will leave in s short while," she replied.

We had gotten to the riverbank. For a moment, I wanted to take the sight in, but I noticed Onyiyechi was nowhere in sight. I panicked.

"Where's Onyiyechi?!" I asked in fear.

"Huh?" Amaka replied. She didn't seem to get it.

"Your sister, where is she?" I asked again. This time Amaka looked around, her eyes expertly roaming and searching.

"Oh my God, what is wrong with this girl? She was just a few steps ahead of us," she replied with a hint of panic in her voice. Mine was full blown.

"Let's look for her and leave this place immediately, please!" I almost yelled.

I wondered why the valley seemed empty at a time like this. Amaka was walk-running by now and I couldn't keep up. I shouted to her to wait for me. She shouted back asking me to stay there while she searched. How on earth was I supposed to stand alone in the fascinating but extremely scary place? I searched around the area looking for clues. My eyes caught footprints about the length of a young girl's feet, so I followed them. Some steps ahead, I saw the clothes Onyiyechi had been wearing hanging on one of the trees, but she was nowhere in sight, nor swimming in the river either. I screamed her name at the top of my voice countless times, but there was no answer.

"I didn't find her," Amaka said as she came up behind me, we were both crying. We kept screaming her name for hours until we decided to go back home at dusk. I was numb. Amaka was crying and fretting. I tried to recall everything that had happened but I couldn't explain anything.

When we got home, we realized people had been sent to look for us. I was still numb. Amaka was telling the tale to the small family crowd that had gathered, with Onyiyechi's clothes dangling in her hands as she gesticulated. A while later, I heard a woman wailing loudly. It was *their mom*, and some people were muttering some things about belonging to the spirit world. I met my dad's disappointed gaze and everything went hazy. I think I fainted but that is all I remember from that night besides the nightmares I had.

We headed back to Lagos the next day, but this time there was nothing fascinating about the road. I had flashes of the whole incident, my sour adventure. *What happened to Onyiyechi? Did she really belong to the spirit world? What exactly does that mean?* I had read similar stories before but presumed they were all mystical and fictional. Now it was all muddled up in my brain. *Would she ever be found?*

My name is Chinecherem. I am now fifteen. You wonder why I write in past tense but these were the events of my first and last trip to my village three years ago. My adventure turned sour at its peak but the trauma remained for months. I have blamed myself these three years for following through with Amaka's idea. I'm coming out slowly and that is why I can write this experience down. Onyiyechi was never found and I never want to go to my village again. At least, not anytime soon.

The Travelling Man

by Radha Zutshi Opubor
A story from Nigeria
First place winner

Eni wondered, sometimes, when she'd meet the Travelling Man. No, that wasn't right. She wondered, sometimes, when the Travelling Man would meet her. She'd met him already. She'd known him half her life.

It was happening more now, the forgetting. There were some things she always knew. Her name was Enitanwa Deem, and she was twenty-eight, and she was tall for a woman. She knew her own face when she saw it in the mirror. She knew that wide, flat nose was her father's, that those dark eyes were her mother's. She knew that in the half-light her skin was so black it was blue, and she knew that Deji was the first person to tell her she was beautiful. But she could not remember marrying him. Sometimes she would blink awake from half-sleep, and he'd be looking at her, and she would think *I don't know him, but his eyes are kind.* A year ago, that thought would have frightened her. She would have said, "Deji," and he'd have held her as they cried. And that night as the sweat cooled on their bodies she'd have stared at his pale-brown face until her eyes burned. And then, again—*I don't know him, but he has sad eyes.* When would he meet her, the Travelling Man? It would have to be soon. In a way, it made sense that she was forgetting. Not to her doctors, or to Deji. They could only see a woman newly-married, glowing with health. But Eni understood. It was simple; her past was bigger than her future, and her mind could not hold it anymore. That was what happened when you were about to die.

It's going to be soon. Eni ran her hand through her curly hair. Gossamer-thin strands came away on her fingers like cobwebs. She was alone in her apartment, and even the Lagos night-noise could not reach her up here. But he could. Eni pulled a heavy blanket around her shoulders and walked to the window. The wide, curving one that let her look out into the lagoon and see the lights on the water. She must've chosen this apartment for that window, small as it was. Eni sat on the floor and let her cheek kiss the glass. It was cool against her skin as she waited for the Travelling Man.

The first time he came to me I was fourteen. I woke in the dead of night and there he was in the window. He was...nineteen, maybe? It was the oldest I ever saw him. It was the youngest he ever saw me. I was skinny and shaking. I slipped out from between my sisters and went over to him, because...because he was crying, and because he was almost gone. He was in the window, half in and half out, and the moonlight shone right through him—turned his skin pale blue. He watched me as I came to him, and he was quiet as he cried. And he said to me, "Shh, don't wake your sisters. I just wanted to see you one last time." He smiled, and the moonlight began taking him to pieces. My heart was in my throat, and I couldn't speak, and so I watched. And just before he was gone, he said—

But Eni couldn't remember. She blinked, and a thin membrane of drool coated her chin, and the window was cold against her forehead. Deji leaned against the wall opposite her, lit by the pinprick lights of their kitchen appliances. That mixer had been on their wedding registry, Eni knew, and it had never been used, not once. His eyes were sad. Eni turned back to the window. She felt Deji as he came to her and took her chin in his hand. It felt warm. It felt alive. He carefully wiped her face clean with his sleeve. "Isoken?" he asked, and the desperation in his voice was well-hidden. Eni shook her head no, she did not know. She suddenly felt that they had done this many times. She would have asked Deji, but he was already pulling away. She kept her face against the window and listened to him leave. It was going to be soon.

"It's the light," he told me, a few months later. It was the second time I saw him. He was dark and alive, not a ghost anymore. No, that's not right. He wasn't a ghost yet. It hadn't happened to him yet, because my past was his future. He told me that, too. I was travelling forwards, and he was travelling backwards. But sometimes, when the light was right, we'd meet. "It's like it takes me apart, and when it puts me together, I'm in your window. Every time I see you, you're younger, and you can't remember the last time I saw you. And now—you haven't met me. So, I won't see you again." I balled my hands into fists, and my nails dug crescent moons into the soft skin of my palms, and they bled. I said nothing, and then I said, "We're friends, aren't we?" because I knew we must be.

He smiled, and said, "I had a sister, once. You and her are the only ones who can see me. She called me the Travelling Man. That's what you'll call me. You and Deji, even though he can't see me." Eni had not known anyone named Deji—although she had met Adedeji, the tall half-caste boy in her English class with the *oyinbo* accent and kind eyes.

The Travelling Man stayed almost two months the second time. One day in the middle of a sentence, the light flared cobalt against his cheekbones. Then he was gone.

When would he meet her? Eni woke in the late afternoon. Yellowing light flooded the apartment. She was curled on the floor, huddled against the window. It took all her strength to lift her head from the floor and sit up against the window. The man was staring at her. Not the Travelling Man, her man. The one with kind eyes. She couldn't remember his name, but Eni knew he was her man. Her body remembered, even if the rest of her didn't. She wanted to cry every time she saw him.

"You should be in a hospital," he said. Eni did not know if there were windows in a hospital, windows with moonlight. She could barely remember the months she spent in the hospital, but she knew that when still-sick people are sent back home, no one expects them to get better. Eni shook her head, no. Deji sighed. He lifted her in his arms as though she weighed nothing and helped her to the bathroom, turned away when she asked him to without words. He said nothing when she returned to the window.

He saw me so many times. For a day, mostly, but often longer, and once for nearly a year. That was a golden year, the year I was engaged to Deji, the year I turned twenty-two. He was the first boy to tell me I was beautiful, and The Travelling Man always knew we'd get married. But I was already forgetting. Little things—cash, my keys. Then bigger ones. I'd forgotten Deji's name that morning, just for an instant. He hadn't noticed. The Travelling Man came to the house after breakfast to see me before I went to work. I was at the kitchen table, waiting for him.

"You know what happens to me, don't you?" I asked. He had been my closest friend for a decade, always happy, always smiling. Reckless, wild. Now he was silent. "Where do you go when you're not here?" I shouted. "Who are you? What's the point of any of it if you won't help me?" The Travelling man was a boy by now—fifteen, growing younger. But suddenly he looked angry, and incredibly ancient.

"You and I travel in different directions. I can only pass through your life backwards, and I can't choose when I come or when I go. I don't know why. It was the same thing with my sister, until one day I knew her and she didn't know me, and I never saw her again. But in all the time when you're not alive, I'm in control. I can go forward or back, see every moment without being seen. I can watch the pyramids go up above me and watch London fall in the War-to-end-all-wars, and when the world burns up—and it will, I've seen that too—and the darkness takes it—"

"Stop it! Stop it, I don't want to hear any more!" I cringed backwards and brought my hands up to cover my face. When the Travelling Man pulled them gently aside, his eyes were wet and tired. He looked impossibly young as he wept into my shoulder.

"I'm so tired," he said. When Deji returned that night, the Travelling Man was gone, and he did not return. And I—

No matter how hard she tried, Eni could not remember a thing before her time in the hospital, when she and Deji had discovered that her body was fading along with her mind. The doctors did not know what had caused the decline of either. Deji had been silent on the way home, his knuckles blue-white against the steering wheel. He had reminded her suddenly of the Travelling Man, and Eni had laughed. It had been too much for him. Deji had pulled the car over to the side of the road, and left the car, and screamed into the night like a demon. And then he came back into the car and kissed Eni until her lips bruised, and he sucked dark marks into her neck for her to remember him by.

Eni blinked. She lay on her back in the blue moonlight. The apartment was at the bottom of the ocean, wreathed in shadow. She could hear Deji's faint breathing from their bedroom, but that did not matter now. The Travelling Man was here. He stepped through her window.

He was perhaps twelve years old, and she had never seen him look so alive nor so old. His eyes were sunken and exhausted, shadowed with black. His back was stooped and his flesh clung tightly to his bones. But the moon still loved him. Blue light filled his hollowed cheeks and caressed his rounded shoulders. As Eni watched, the light reached his eyes and soothed them, and he smiled at her.

"How?" Eni asked. It was clear he knew who she was, but it was also clear that this was the last time she would ever see him. How could they meet again? She could feel herself dying. Every beat of her heart was a struggle. It fluttered in her chest like a bird in a steel trap, growing weaker as it traveled from life into death. So, this is what was to become of her and the boy she loved like her own brother. He'd known this all along and never told her. When they danced through the night in her college dorm room, he saw her here as she lay dying. When he appeared, suddenly, in the colored panes of the stained-glass window in the church at her father's funeral, he'd known one day he'd find her here. It was strange, dying like this. Most people were afraid of losing what they had. Eni felt only longing. She couldn't remember what she was losing, and so it barely felt like a loss. But it would have been nice, here at the end, to have something to want to live for. The Travelling Man squeezed Eni's hand, brought her back. His hand was cold. But it was alive, and that was good.

"You're going to live," he said, "and you're going to see me again. Not too many times—you lose your sight as another gains it. But you *will* see me again. And I'll see you—I'm traveling back to your beginning, growing older all the time. Our friendship...that's all in front of *me*. But that doesn't mean your life ends here. I know it doesn't. I've seen it." The Travelling Man smiled at some secret joke, then continued.

"I've met lots of myselves, from other times. They told me what I had to do, who you are to me. I've been...not quite human, the past few thousand years. Since the moment I was born, I've been going to all times, all places, awaiting the moment I got to meet you *here*. A few of us Travelling Men found a way to save you." The Travelling Man knelt at Eni's side and helped her to sit up with her back to the window. His fingers were callused and worn in hers, hard-used. His hand felt light and insubstantial in hers.

"I'm travelling soon," he said, and he smiled apologetically. Eni's head slumped back against the window. She felt a heat in her chest, a constriction. Her toes began to go numb. The blue shadows in the room lengthened.

"At the very edge of the universe, just before the great contraction where all there is becomes all there will be, I found something for you. A...late wedding present. Here," the Travelling Man said, opening his hand. In it was a small blue tear, a chip of ice, shining slightly with an inward light. "It's time," he said. "Nearly forty years of it, suspended. And it's yours." He pressed it into Eni's palm, but her hand fell open. She could no longer feel her body. She no longer knew she was Eni Deem, tall for a woman. But she knew, still, her Travelling Man.

"This will freeze you—a loop in time, but you'll be the only one it catches. Travelling forward, untouched by time, untouched by illness. Unmoored like me, but going in the right direction, until it runs out and you start at the beginning, not knowing you've done it before. I didn't just find this; it's worth more than the earth. Someone gave this to me. He'd fought for eons to get it, fought some of the worst beings the galaxy had to offer, and he was fading. He told me to give this to you. He had one more stop to make before he was gone."

Eni breathed in, a small noise of surprise. Her Travelling Man smiled. He clasped Eni's hand closed around the jewel. It froze against her palm. The cold shocked her senses, like crashing into a frozen sea.

"We'll see each other again. I'm in your past now, Eni. But you're my future. Every time I see you now, you'll be younger." The Travelling Man had begun to cry, and the blue tear-tracks cut his face into pieces. His voice was oddly thick when he spoke again.

"I just...I want you to know that I'm going to be all right. I grew up in some strange places and some strange times. I sort of raised myself. But I had my sister. I got to travel to her for half her life. I won't see her again, but she hasn't even met me yet. She hasn't even named me the Travelling Man." The Travelling Man leaned forward and kissed Eni's cheek. In the burning cold, thoughts crystallized one after another. Eni remembered Deji. She remembered—

The light pulled the Travelling Man apart. The crystal in Eni's palm melted, and her mind froze, and she felt it as time lost its hold on her. All the strings inside her shattered in the sudden cold, and she remembered.

"Isoken," I said when I was twenty-five, clutching my newborn daughter all wrong but afraid to let her go even for a moment. "One who is contented with her destiny," Deji echoed, and laughed. "Unlike her mother." It was later that year I forgot her on the changing table in a supermarket and Deji began to ask me, "Isoken?" And it was the year after that when I began to shake my head no, and he sent her to live with her grandmother.

Eni moaned. The longing for her daughter came upon her all at once, and she almost would not bear it. She began to stand, to wake Deji, to drive sleep-addled to her mother's house and find her child. How could she not have remembered her daughter? She knew everything about her—her warm brown skin, her curly hair, her small round teeth. Eni knew she'd give her the skin off her arms if she had to, the bones out of her legs. But her knees buckled as she tried to stand, and she fell under the weight of one last memory. Her mind washed blue, and Eni saw.

I was fourteen, and he was in the window, half in and half out, and the moonlight shone right through him—turned his skin pale blue. He watched me as I came to him, and he was quiet as he cried. And he said to me, "Shh, don't wake your sisters. I just wanted to see you one last time." He smiled, and the moonlight began taking him to pieces. My heart was in my throat, and I couldn't speak, and so I watched. And just before he was gone, he said—

"Mom."

Eni felt a small fluttering in her stomach as the child inside her travelled for the first time, and was gone.

Chronicle Of A Village Girl

By Wilmah Kudakwashe Mupa

A story from Zimbabwe

Part 1

Mazambuko village was located on the outskirts of Masvingo, a city in Zimbabwe. Apart from its breathtaking nature, it was also the only village known for its rivers which never dried up, and brisk waters. Different people from different villages would always come to Mazambuko whenever drought struck. Our chief, Chief Zadza was a very noble and honest man, filled with great humanity as well as a strong compassion especially for widows and orphans. " Bonjour my daughter," he would always say whenever he would see me. It so happened that on a certain day he came looking for my father and was exhilarated by my strong passion for reading. He had found me seated by our kitchen door and reading a French book, which was translated to English. "Teach me one word, my daughter, "he said. "Bonjour is a way of greeting sir," I responded and from that day, we would always greet each other in French.

Growing up, I had always had a strong passion for reading, hoping that one day I would become an author. The thrills I would get from reading literally anything I would set my eyes on were just something unexplainable. From newspapers to magazines to novels, I would read anything and everything. It astounded me how authors, especially novelists would bring something right out of their imagination or experience to formulate the ideal literature that would captivate the hearts of readers, myself included. On top of that, being able to decipher another writer's work was another feeling that encouraged me that this was also definitely supposed to by my thing. "One day is one day," I would always say to myself. I always pictured several books authored by myself. It was my dream.

Society would somehow make children like us feel somewhat inferior, as if there was nothing we were ever going to achieve in life, and by children like us I mean those that were being raised by single parents. For as long as I can remember, my father had played both parental roles since I was a kid. Often he captured precious moments since I was a toddler. Each and every time I would look at some of the pictures which hung on the walls, I felt loved. He always made sure that I had everything that I needed, regardless of our situation. He had been my rock ever since the day my mother decided to keep me a secret when she married another man. Since the day she left us, she only came to visit me once, apparently. I was still young then. From then onwards, her whereabouts were just rumoured all over the village. Some said she relocated to Mozambique, some said she was scared that her husband would find out about me and so on. I couldn't care less honestly. Life goes on and it was going on perfectly fine without her.

Part 2

"Bring some tomatoes on your way back," my father shouted as I exited through the kitchen door. Today marked a fortnight since I wrote my final Advanced Level examinations. My results were going to define whether I would proceed to university or not. Ah yes! University, the place of my dreams! My father had started saving up from the day I completed my Ordinary Level in school. My dream was to study creative writing. It was everyone's dream that I proceeded to college and so I always looked forward to it. The paternal side of my family had very high hopes for me and I was not planning on disappointing them.

Theresa and I were going to spend some time together at the river. This was our go-to spot whenever we felt like venting to each other about how life was treating us, and our hopes for the future. Her dream was to be an accountant. Theresa and I had been friends since kindergarten. She came from a lovely home and her parents were so friendly and forthcoming. They made me feel like one of their own children. We made our way to the river as the autumn winds whipped past us. We made several stops just to admire the beauty that nature offers and it stalled us from getting to the river. The mountainous rocks aligned vertically and gave an ethereal appearance. The birds chirped melodiously from one tree to the other, alerting us that a splendid day awaited us.

Eventually we got to the river. Was I dreaming or was I not? I could not believe my eyes as I sat by the rock. "Theresa!" I shouted in disbelief. I stood still, gawking at the sight. To say I was dreaming would not be convincing because my toes were partly immersed in water and I could feel its coldness, giving me the assurance that this was, indeed, real. It seemed as though Theresa did not hear me calling her. Perhaps I was inaudible so I shouted again, louder this time. "Theresa!" and she came. We stood there in disbelief. "But who could have left it there?" Theresa asked. By the side of the rock were two separate 50 USD notes from the United States of America. Gracious Lord! "My friend, we need to go with the money to the chief so that he can make an announcement all around the village. Perhaps someone dropped it when they came to the river." I suggested. We headed off to the chief to leave the money which we had found. On my way back home I was still in shock. I had never seen such a huge amount of money. I've only read about 100 USD. Now seeing it, that was definitely something else. Another indescribable feeling, and so there I was, sunk deep in thought. I was brought back to reality when I approached our garden and in that moment my father's words replayed in my mind. Ah yes! Tomatoes for my dearest papa. I picked a plastic bag-full. Eventually I got home and informed my father about the incident which took place at the river. Just like me, he was also shocked.

Part 3

A few days later the chief called in to notify us that there was no one from the village who came to claim that money, so we might as well have it. Call it fortune, call it luck, but the money was, in fact, ours to keep. Theresa and I looked at the chief in disbelief. What were we going to do with 100 USD in a small village like ours? "Mavis, we can go buy lots of food and clothes from the stores," Theresa suggested. Theresa honestly had so many ideas in regard to how we were going to spend the money. I, on the other hand, had a completely different idea from all of hers. I wanted to give it to my father so he could add it up to my college money, which he had been saving up for over the past couple of years.

I went back home to tell my father that I had 50 USD. Theresa and I had divided the money in half. Being the superstitious and traditional man that he is, my father sprinkled some salt onto the money. "We do not know where the money came from, my daughter, so we should get rid of all the bad luck," he said. I could not help but laugh. I found this not only hilarious, but dramatic as well. My father was a true traditional African man after all. To my surprise, he suggested that I keep the money for my personal use and that he did not need me helping him with saving for college. He was adamant about it so I was left with no choice but to keep the money! It was at that point that I discovered that all these incidents were simply directing me to something new, the beginning of something I never pictured myself doing, the sudden start of an adventure.

That night I went to bed thinking of how I had actually never been to the capital city of my own country. Well matter of fact, I used to go there, but as a kid so I do not remember much, so it actually does not count. I needed to explore any part of that big city now that I was a little grown up. Before you knew it, I was already planning to go for a trip to Harare! The next morning I went to inform Theresa about my sudden interest in travelling to Harare. She was nonchalant about the idea but I was very much eager to go, with or without her.

Part 4

After three days of thorough research on Harare and planning, I took my bags and headed off to the bus station where I boarded the bus to Harare. The only relative I knew there was my father's older brother who was a Headmaster at a certain school whose name I didn't actually know. My father directed me where to board buses to his house, once I got to Harare. Everything was going on fine until I went to the given address once I got to Harare only to be told that my uncle had moved. I stood by the gate as I felt my whole body sweating profusely because I did not have anywhere else to go to. I was so devastated and had not anticipated this. I was frantic! Oh well, this meant that I had no other option but to go back home. How disappointing! What of the things I wanted to explore in Harare? My adventure was already coming to an end before it even commenced.

I was still trying to gain my composure when a car arrived and parked right next door. A man who looked in his late 20s from what I could tell from his physical appearance got out of the car and looked at me like he knew me. "Mavis," he called out my name. "It's Mavis right?" he asked. I honestly had no idea who this man was but I did confirm my name.

"I can see you do not remember me. I am Matthew and we used to play together whenever you visited your uncle," he said. "And you have not changed much Mavis," he added. Well last time I was said to have visited my uncle I was only four years old so it only made sense that I did not recall much. Matthew was very friendly, I must say. It was a pity I did not remember him so it felt like I was actually meeting him for the first time. I asked him if he knew where my uncle had relocated to. Lucky for me he did. He wrote down the address for me and I could not be any happier. He gave me his numbers too and asked that I call him when I get there. Matthew was leaving Zimbabwe that night on a business trip. Oh, how I envied him! Matthew's parents, who were my uncle's neighbours then had moved to South Africa and were renting out that house they used to live in. So it turned out that Matthew had come to collect rental payments when he found me stranded. Apart from being friendly, I also found Matthew to be very attractive and the fact that he came to my rescue, well it was in that moment that I felt like I had found me a knight in shining armour. Just the way I read it in several novels.

Harare is actually a very large city, I must say. The skyscrapers in the CBD were something I had never seen, even in my imagination. They were breathtaking. The people in the city have a different way of living as compared to those back at the village. City life is indeed a fast life. Lots of cars, buildings, vendors and so on. Eventually I got to the place where my uncle had relocated to. I was going to stay there for a maximum of three days and hoped to engage in various outdoor activities. I mean, this was Harare! The big city! And all my life I lived in a village.

With a huge grin on my face, I knocked on the gate as I anticipated to be welcomed by either of my cousins, aunt or uncle. To my surprise, a very stern male figure appeared and asked me to follow him. It seemed as though he was expecting someone of both my gender and age. I tried to tell him my story, but he seemed aloof and a bit distracted.

"So young lady, you are telling me that you are not the person I spoke to earlier on?"

"Definitely not sir," I responded politely.

Part of me was frightened too. I mean this man could be a serial killer or a rapist for all I knew. I had heard of how such kind of people operate, especially in Harare, and with the atmosphere that came with this man, everything about him pointed to him being a bad guy. I started to fear for my life.

There was another knock on the gate and this man attended to it as the village girl in me took the opportunity to stare around his house like mad. It was indeed a huge house, and beautiful too though the paintings which hung by the wall were very....disturbing if I may say so. There were pictures of creepy creatures and things of that sort. Perhaps for the people that lived in the city it was just basic art, but for me, this was...evil. Several thoughts battled in my mind as I wondered what business this man could possibly be in. I was brought back to reality when I heard footsteps approaching closer and closer to where I was seated. Behind this man was another girl who looked my age. I concluded that that must be the person this man had mistaken me for. Meanwhile I was very stressed out. I felt like crying and especially after knowing that Matthew might not be able to help me since he was leaving the country.

Part 5

My uncle's whereabouts were unknown and I had no means whatsoever of communicating with my father back at the village. If push came to shove, I was going to beg this man to let me stay in his house for the night. Since there was another female figure, I felt a little less scared even though the thought of having to spend the night in this house still made me cringe. All these thoughts kept running in my head before this man and the girl eventually got to the room where I was.

It turned out this man was one of the most prestigious businessmen in Harare and he had no family. He also had been looking for a helper for his house and the young lady whose name I got to know was Mariah was actually going to be one. My head cleared off when I actually realised that I had once read about this man in a business class back in high school. I was safe! He was harmless. He offered for me to stay the night since it was getting dark, and the following day he would help me look for my uncle. And it was in that moment that I felt very lucky. What was I going to do? I was pretty much stranded and what came out to be the wrong address turned out to be a blessing in disguise too. Both Mariah and I were unfamiliar with the house so Mr. Abrahams gave us a tour. His home was even bigger than I thought!

I woke up in the middle of the night to use the bathroom as I bumped into Mr. Abrahams, holding a coffee mug and a briefcase. I concluded that being the businessman that he is, he was probably just working late. "Everything alright, Mavis?" he asked out of concern. I assured him that I was fine and just needed to use the bathroom. I was careful to use the bathroom just the way Mr. Abrahams instructed us to when he gave us the house tour. But now that I was operating the equipment myself, the feeling was even more thrilling. The sinks splashed out hot water too and the hand dryer let out warm air. It was quite chilly so I then asked myself to take this opportunity to...you know...heat up my whole body. So I bent down under the dryer as the warm air blew on my skin, making me feel so warm. For a village girl like me, this was heaven! I had never seen this in my whole entire life so you can just imagine the excitement which came from having had this experience, as well as being able to brag at the people back home. This was indeed my Christmas, my birthday, my heaven on earth and every other ceremonial event you can think of.

I was woken up the following day by the sound of the gate which opened for a very luxurious car that was entering Mr. Abrahams premises. I stood by the window, and my jaw dropped as I stared at this wonderful car. A male authoritative-looking figure came out and Mr. Abrahams left with him. It then occurred to me that I had to go back home. During that evening, Mr. Abrahams was surprisingly open to talk about other things beyond my search for my uncle. He mentioned that I had great ambitions and yet I still felt that my Advanced Level results held my fate.

"I tell you what, why don't you take my contact details and address. If your results come in and you performed well, I am guaranteeing you both work and school to further your studies, so you can come back to Harare."

I sat there in awe! This man was heaven sent. To think that my father had been saving up and yet all along I was meant to meet Mr. Abrahams! I was so grateful and also prayed hard that when my results came in, they would take me to the next level in my life which I had been hoping for all these years. Soon my mother would be reading about me in the newspapers and she would regret the day she abandoned me. My imagination ran far.

Part 6

The next day I said my goodbyes to my new friend Mariah, Mr. Abraham's helper. I did say to her that we would meet soon again. Mr. Abrahams took me to the bus station where I boarded the bus back to Mazambuko village. In four hours' time I arrived home to celebrations. It turned out that while I was in Harare, my results came in and Theresa had gone to collect for me since I was absent. The school required any of my parents' consent in order for another student to collect my results on my behalf. So Theresa had taken with her a letter from my father, which had his signature and collected both our results. Our dreams were becoming more and more real. I told my friends about my adventure and about the promises Mr. Abrahams had made to me. Theresa could not stop laughing about my experience with the hand dryer. She longed to see the things I had seen in Harare. My father was very proud of me, and so were the rest of my family.

I spent another week at home before heading back to Harare.

My father was very sad to be left alone but happy at the same time that I was pursuing my goals, just as I wanted to. I was over the moon as I made my way to Harare. It felt as if what awaited me was again, another commencement of something I had never pictured to be that way, the start of yet another adventure!

"Life is either a daring adventure, or nothing. To keep our faces toward change and behave like free spirits in the presence of fate is strength undefeatable" – Helen Keller.

Ifechukwu

By Favour Modekwe
A story from Nigeria
Second place winner

My name is Ifechukwu Okonkwo. I am the last of six children. Know that I am special and loved because I am the only female child of my parents. I am blessed with dimples when I smile. Like my mother, I've got a lovely set of white teeth. I love my siblings especially my immediate elder brother Sopuruchi; he is very talented and the most handsome among my brothers. In my family, beauty is a gift that nature has bestowed on us. Legend has it that our parents were created on 'Eke,' which is market day, and were blessed by the python goddess to possess her enchantment and beauty.

My mum Nnedi in her prime was the beauty of the village and had many admirers and suitors, but she kept rejecting them.

One day she went to the market to sell vegetables. The market was a big one. The neighbouring villages also came to the market to trade. On that beautiful day she placed her wares on the mat she had spread on the ground, and she started alerting customers to her direction. Suddenly, she saw the young man who would eventually become my father and became as though struck by lightning. She stood and gazed agape until flies entered into her mouth. She came to her senses when one of the flies also perched on her eye. That was when she looked away and cautioned herself.

We the children always laughed hard about the marriage of our parents because our father also told us that he had followed our mum sheepishly that day after the close of the market to find out where she lived. He said that he was mesmerized by her beauty and wanted to marry her. But he did not know what her reaction would be, so he decided to follow her from a safe distance.

Trouble escalated when it rained heavily on their way home and he couldn't find a place to hide from the rain. He thought he had come to the end of his misery when the rain stopped but was faced with worse situation because when he stood up, he realized that it was already dark and he couldn't find his way back. He decided to continue following them from behind until they got to my mother's compound. He wanted to be so close to her that he decided to sleep on the ground near my mother's window. Eventually at midnight he was not only drenched again with rain but bathed with the urine of almost everyone in the family. The only thing he escaped from was the soldier ants and like he would say "the gods took pity on me." Early in the morning, when my mother woke up to fetch her water pot, she screamed when she saw the cold body of the young man. Her pot shattered into pieces and the noise attracted the whole family. All of them were surprised to see this handsome young man in their compound. But my mum explained that she had seen him in the market. In her words, she said,

"Finally the gods have brought him to me. Praise be the gods. "

These words left the whole family in awe because they couldn't understand how their precious daughter they had been begging to get married was elated by a half-dead man. The family decided to get to the root of the matter later but first they had to save the life of the young man, so they carried him in and soaked him with herbs until he recovered. Unfortunately, that marked the introduction and finally the marriage of my parents.

This morning while the moon was still smiling down on us, my mum woke me up early to accompany her to the village stream. She wanted me to help with doing the laundry. I was still angry she woke me up from a beautiful dream where I was being crowned the queen of our great kingdom. The prospect of going to the village stream early in the morning during the rainy season, walking through those bushy paths and listening to weird sounds from nocturnal creatures was not a palatable idea.

"Ifechukwu" my mother roared, "what are you still doing standing like a foolish goat? Better carry that basket of clothes and let's go."

While she soliloquized about our lateness, I followed behind her with the basket on my head, grumbling. I was always asking my *chi* why I came out as a girl instead of a boy. My brothers were still sleeping, they would still follow papa to the farm but that would be later. They always enjoyed better sleep while I didn't. If I could, I would have changed my gender and enjoyed a few more hours sleeping. Onyedika, our parents' first born, had promised to help me change my gender if I stayed still when he let the centipede sting me. My foolish mind had agreed to that idea because I've heard people refer to the centipede as *gbalunwokeghonwanyi*, which means that after it stings, it changes a man into a woman because of how its sting makes a boy scream like a girl. It was a lie and I learnt the truth in a painful way. I let my brother play his cruel trick on me. I cried not just because of the sting but because it seemed like my dream of being a male had been destroyed. It was later I discovered that it was payback for the day I ate his food while he slept. He woke up very hungry that night and cried until he cried himself to sleep.

"Ifechukwu!" My mother called again. We had already gotten to the stream, and I was sitting down on a stone to regain the energy I spent walking to the stream. The stream was already filled with women fetching water, washing bitter leaf, washing clothes, while other women were taking their bath. I busied myself with the clothes I was rinsing for my mum when Mrs. Okeke came to gossip with my mum. It was rumored that the village priestess wanted to hand over to a younger person who would take over from her. It was required that every family would present one of their daughters. These girls would go to the shrine for some time until the priestess found the chosen one through a process of elimination. The elimination process was so deadly that it involved death, madness or blindness and other injuries to the girl that may render the child useless. This contest frightened mama and I saw her face was filled with fear. I kept myself busy with the clothes I was washing while I thought about the contest.

The contest was an old tradition which the gods used in selecting a worthy maiden to serve as a seer and a mediator between the villagers and the gods. The contest was last done many years ago even before the birth of our parents. My grandmother had told me very scary tales of how deadly and adventuresome the contest was. Anybody who won the contest became the priestess and had same power as the king of the land. The priestess would serve the gods and the people all the days of her life until she became old, then she would prepare for a new contest in order to get a successor. The priestess who was my grandmother's age had decided to select a new priestess and a young one too. Who would have thought that the contest was going to be hold in our time? I wondered with mixed feelings what was in store for us.

That night my mother told my father about the contest and papa was not happy with it. He began to make plans to sneak me out to my mother's village. But unfortunately for us, the kingdom guards showed up very early to take one girl from each family. When they came to my house, Onyedika told me he wished the millipede sting had worked. I would have been a male and no one would have come to our house. I cried louder when he told me this. Mama cried uncontrollably as if I was already dead. Everyone accompanied us to the shrine where the priestess and the king were waiting. The king calmed everyone down and promised everyone that this year would not involve any death or casualties. This time around all the girls would be fortified and given a task. Anyone who found favour in the sight of the gods would become the new priestess.

After the king's speech, the crowd cheered and applauded. They were greatly pleased that the future of their sisters and daughters was still safe and would not be cut short. Some of us who were still crying dried our tears and smiled at our parents and siblings. Everyone was relieved after the king's speech. Our parents were also assured that we would be taken care of and we would enjoy the contest. After this, our parents were asked to say their goodbyes. When our parents left, we all sat down in front of the priestess waiting for instructions.

The priestess, Ada-Agbara (Agbara being a deity), was a short, dark woman with a scary look. Merely looking at her face could frighten the living daylights out of you. She was not only strict but highly disciplined. She gave out many more instructions than I could even remember because I was so hungry. After giving us instructions, she counted us and discovered we were forty-two in number, so she divided us into seven groups of seven. Each group had a day to cook, clean, dance, play, answer questions, and sing. We would train for a period of seven days. After which we would compete among ourselves and only the best group would be fortified and would go into the forest. After the orientation we were given a bowl of hot *akpu* (a meal prepared by pounding hot cassava) and another bowl of hot *egusi* (melon seed) soup garnished with dry meat for dinner. We all ate happily and turned in for the night.

The next day every group woke up and came together at the *obi*. The priestess Ada-Agbara advised each group to choose a team leader. Ezinne was chosen to lead my group because she was the oldest in our group and seemed more organized than all of us. The others were Mmesoma, Adanna, Egodi, and the one whom I become fast friends with, Uchenna.

The day's activities began with sweeping and tidying up the place. Our group was given a portion to sweep and the portion had a very large mango tree in it. I wanted to pluck some mangoes but Ezinne refused to let us touch anything. After sweeping, we started going back to the *obi* only to realize there was a goat bleating loudly and following us. The most surprising thing was that the goat was wearing Adanna's clothes. We began to search for Adanna but she was nowhere to be found. It was then that the priestess appeared and told us that Adanna had stolen and eaten some mangoes, and now she was suffering the consequences of her action. Ezinne knelt down and pleaded on her behalf. We also joined in begging the priestess until she had pity on Adanna and turned her back. This incident was a very clear warning to us and we all took notice.

Our subsequent activities started with practice on singing and dancing. I was the black sheep of the group because I could neither sing nor dance. I had to join those playing drums as Uchenna had promised to teach me the steps. We danced, sang and listened to stories of the ancient days until Ujunwa began to shout and roll all over the floor. We did not know what was wrong with her until Ada-Agbara deduced that she had gone to steal more food after everyone had eaten. She was administered some herbs and sent away. Ada-Agbara stated that she had forgiven Adanna because she had not warned us about stealing from her earlier, but henceforth anyone who violated the rules would suffer the consequence and would be sent away. This caused a heavy silence among us until we retired to bed.

The seven days continued. I had learnt to sing and dance thanks to Uchenna who took the pains of teaching me. On the seventh day we all woke up anxious and excited; we were about to learn what lay in store for us. Ezinne had been a good leader; she had taught us comportment and carriage. She had also taught us on how to smile while dancing and how to ignore distractors while dancing. So many times Ezinne would tease me by saying "Ifechukwu, better smile well so that your beauty and dimples can help us win." I would smile heartily and tell her that only the gods can choose.

At soon as it was time to display what we had learnt, all the villagers gathered in front of the shrine to watch us and see the winners. I was very shy and scared when I saw the crowd but Egodi encouraged me. We were the last group to perform and watching others perform, I thought we might never have a chance. Finally we got to the stage and danced. The crowd cheered so much and I saw myself and our group dancing so well. The crowd applauded us and the Priestess after all the dances declared that our group had won.

This marked the end of the practice and the start of the journey into the strange forest. That night, the priestess soaked us in strong smelly herbs and told us to take our baths with those herbs. We were given strong concoctions to drink. We were given also white wrappers to tie, which was a symbol of peace and purity. Ada-Agbara congratulated us once again. She said, "Only the pure and kind-hearted are chosen by the gods, and you all are. You are to find the *Ofo* (staff that signifies authority.

41

It is often wielded by titled men or the priest or priestess) in the forest. Anyone who comes back with the *Ofo* is chosen." At midnight she took us to the mouth of the forest and prayed for the spirits to guide us. She gave us a jar of water and some fruit which we put in our small bags. She warned us not to eat anything in the forest before she bade us goodbye and watched us walk into the forest.

The first day was uneventful as we walked deep into the forest aimlessly but searching for the *Ofo*. When it started to get dark, we found some shade under a big tree and we lay down. By midnight we started hearing the drums playing hard. We all woke up looking for the source of the music but we couldn't find it. Yet the music continued to grow louder. All of a sudden, Uchenna could no longer control herself because she loved music. She began to dance vigorously while Ezinne tried to warn her to stop. She danced until she disappeared. We all ran away out of fright. Soon Egodi also started laughing loud and started dancing. We tried to hold her but she too disappeared. We held ourselves tightly and continued deep into the forest until we got tired and fell asleep under a tree.

When we woke up, we saw that the tree under which we slept had fruits of different colors and they looked very appetizing. We remembered the warning of 'Ada-Agbara' not to eat anything but Adanna jumped up, plucked one of the fruits and ate it. She immediately turned into a multicolored masquerade and began to chase us. We screamed and ran for our dear lives until we looked back and saw that she had disappeared. We stopped running and sat down on a rock to rest. Suddenly the rock began to move. We looked down to see that the rock had turned into a tortoise. We ran until we got to the stream. Mmesoma was panting heavily. Our water jar was already exhausted yet we could not drink from the forest. Ezinne tried encouraging us not to drink any water from the forest no matter how thirsty we got. Suddenly, Mmesoma jumped up and shouted, "I would rather die in the water than die of thirst." We saw her rush into the stream to slake her thirst and, before our eyes, the stream turned to blood and we no longer saw Mmesoma.

The *Ofo* was nowhere to be found and yet we were almost dead. Just then we saw a glowing white hut which caught our interest. As we got closer, we saw two stools and each stool had an *Ofo* placed on it. Suddenly an old woman appeared and said to us, "My daughters you have gotten to the last destination. Each stool has a different *Ofo* placed on it. One is fake and the other is the original, so choose wisely."

After saying this, she disappeared. As we got closer, I told Ezinne that we could take both of them. Only the person who got the original would be Priestess but at least it would end our suffering. But as I was still talking, Ezinne pushed me down and hit me with a big stick. She said to me, "Do you think I came here to go back with you? I didn't suffer for nothing. I must be the custodian of the original *Ofo* from today." She rushed to pick both of them. Suddenly the stools began to burn and also burnt Ezinne in the process. I was too tired to save her so I watched her burn till she disappeared.

I sat down confused and tried to regain my strength. The stools and the *Ofo* had been destroyed. What then was the fate of my people? I began to cry for my people when the old woman suddenly appeared again and wiped my tears. She introduced herself as the goddess the land served. She said that she had chosen me to be the custodian of the *Ofo* because I had a good heart and also had the people in mind. She stretched out her hand and gave me the *Ofo*. I accepted it from her and began to yell, "Thank you, great goddess. Thank you, great goddess."

Just then I heard my brother shouting my name and shaking my shoulder. I woke up only to realize I had been dreaming. The last thing I heard was my mum telling my dad about the contest. When they asked me why I was yelling in my sleep, I told them my dreams and they laughed hard at me. Still trying to wrap my mind around the dream I just had, I heard papa say, "The contest cannot hold like that anymore because the Christians have condemned the shrine of Agbara. Only the idol worshippers would attend." My brothers reminded me that the culture was barbaric and people were no longer willing to sacrifice their children for such customs.

I stood outside gazing at the sun while my brothers left for the farm. Once again I remembered how much I wanted to be a boy.

The Magic Clay Pot

By Ifeyinwa Ogwo
A story from Nigeria
Third place winner

Long ago, in a village called Akam in the eastern part of Nigeria, West Africa, lived a girl named Aku, her mother named Ulo, and her little brother named Ani. Aku was a very beautiful, kind, honest, and obedient girl, who would deprive herself of frolicking with other girls of her age group to fend for her mother and little brother. At the age of nine, Aku lost her father, a brave hunter, to a strange disease that struck the village, leaving ten persons dead. Since then Ulo took up the responsibility of taking care of her two children without support from her husband's kinsmen who took over all her husband possessions and drove them out of their house to live in a little hut in the forest on the outskirts of the village. Ulo resorted to menial jobs such as fetching firewood and water, and farming for those that hired her services, to sustain her family.

When Aku approached the age of sixteen, she began accompanying her mother to do the menial jobs, as well as engaging in trading rabbits, squirrels, birds and guinea fowl caught from her trap. She would give the little money she realized from the sale of the game to her mother to support their upkeep. Irrespective of their poor living conditions, Aku never refused to provide food or water to any stranger that lost their way in the forest. She always told her mother, "There is joy in giving, and I know that the gods of our land will answer all our prayers one day."

The village of Akam had a king called Egbe who had a son called Ike and three daughters named Nwanma, Ego and Oledo. Since the death of his queen, the king had refused to remarry, and his three daughters were married to different princes. King Egbe was a very powerful, strict and a rich man, who ruled his subjects with an iron fist. Although he was not a wicked king, the people were afraid of him because of his strict, powerful and humorless demeanor.

One day, a strange illness struck Prince Ike, King Egbe's son, and the king summoned every herbalist in the village to his palace. The herbalists administered their herbs to Prince Ike, but his health kept deteriorating. King Egbe became sad and worried because of the strange sickness ravaging his only son and heir to the throne. He summoned the Chief Priest of the village to his palace to ascertain what could be done to save his son's life. Upon his arrival at the palace, the Chief Priest performed some rituals and chanted some incantations to the gods of the land. The Chief Priest then told King Egbe that his son could only be saved if he drank water from a magic clay pot from the land of the dead.

"This task is a great and difficult one which will only be carried out by a girl with a pure heart," he said.

The king was perturbed by the demands of the gods because he didn't know where to find the girl with a pure heart. He inquired from the Chief Priest whom among the girls in the village could undertake such heavy task.

The Chief Priest told him, "Go to the forest on the outskirts of the village and you will see a hut. In that hut, lives a girl called Aku with her mother and little brother. Bring them to the palace. Please, do not send your guard to seek them out. The gods said you should carry out the mission by yourself. I will await your return."

Early in the morning, King Egbe set out for the forest on the outskirts of the village dressed like a farmer, as the Chief Priest had advised. When he got to the hut, there was no one at home. He sat on a fallen tree trunk to wait for their return. At midday, after they had finished their menial jobs, Aku, her mother and little brother arrived home and found King Egbe waiting, disguised as a farmer. They greeted him and gave him food to eat, not knowing he was the king. After the meal, King Egbe asked Ulo why they lived in the forest by themselves. Ulo narrated the treatment they received from her late husband's kinsmen and the menial jobs they did for a living. King Egbe invited Ulo to live in his farmhouse and work for him, noting that he would pay them handsomely and restore all her husband's properties back to her. Ulo accepted the offer and thanked King Egbe for his kindness.

They set out in the morning for the "farmhouse." On arriving at the palace, Ulo became afraid and asked King Egbe why they were stopping at the palace. King Egbe revealed his true self to them.

"Do not be afraid. I will not hurt you; neither have you committed any crime that is punishable. I need your daughter's help to save the life of my only son. Please do not refuse me your daughter's help."

Ulo promised to allow her daughter to help his son without knowing the task her daughter would undertake. Then, King Egbe took Ulo and Aku to the Chief Priest, who informed them of what Aku needed to do to save the king's son. Ulo and Aku began to cry but since she had promised Aku's help, she consoled Aku noting that the gods of their land would guide her to land of the dead and bring her back safely with the magic clay pot.

The Chief Priest gave Aku a piece of white chalk, a cowry bangle to wear on her wrist, nuts to eat whenever she got hungry, and three little pebbles. He instructed Aku,

"Eat these nuts whenever you are hungry. They will sustain you throughout the journey. Rub the white chalk on any wounds you incur on the journey. Do not remove the cowry bangle from your wrist for any reason. Throw a pebble on the ground whenever you sense danger. But through it all, your pure and kind heart will lead you safely. Do not eat any fruit in the land of the dead except when directed to by a kind spirit. Go well my daughter."

Aku set off for the land of the dead. When she got to the boundary between the living and dead, she met a feeble old woman who had a heavy load on her head. She walked up to the old woman and said,

"Please, may I help you with your load, Ma?"

The old woman allowed her to help her and they walked a very long and rough road, but Aku never complained about the weight of the load. She tagged along behind the old woman until they got to her hut. The old woman offered to let Aku to stay the night with her and asked where she was going. Aku narrated her mission to the old woman who, after listening, gave Aku a bamboo flute.

"Blow this flute whenever you encounter difficulty. It will produce a beautiful melodic music that will lead you to your goal."

Aku thanked the old woman and put the gift in her goatskin bag. She prepared food for the old woman and herself to eat. After eating, they retired to the mat to sleep.

In the morning, she swept the old woman's hut, fetched some firewood and water, and prepared a meal for her before proceeding on her journey. When she entered the land of the dead, she encountered a demon with two big heads and large eyes. The demon stopped her with a bark.

"What are you doing here and who authorized you to come here?"

"My name is Aku. I am here to collect the magic clay pot. Please could you direct me where to get it?" she replied.

The demon became furious that Aku spoke back to him boldly, so he charged towards her. Immediately, Aku brought out the bamboo flute and started playing it. The sweet melody from the bamboo flute caused the demon to dance joyfully. He danced and danced and danced until he became tired. He looked at Aku kindly saying,

"You are a brave girl to come to the land of the dead for the magic clay pot. May I ask what you need the magic clay pot for?"

Aku told the two-headed demon the reason she needed the

magic clay pot. He gave her three kernels of corn and told her,

"You will cross three rivers. At each river, throw these corn kernels and say, 'Let me through, please.' When you have crossed the last river, you will see a tree on its banks. Pluck three ripe fruits from it and lick it. Do not look back whenever you cross the rivers," he warned her.

Aku thanked him and continued on her journey. Before she got to the first river, a tree branch struck her arm and she began to bleed. She immediately remembered the piece of white chalk given to her by the Chief Priest. She drew a circle with it on her wound and the bleeding stopped immediately. When she arrived at the first river, she threw one of the corn kernels given to her by the demon into the river and said, "Let me through, please." The river parted into two and created a narrow path for her to cross. Despite the noises she heard behind her, she didn't look back but kept on moving until she got to the other side of the river. As she continued her journey, a horrifying bull with three heads and red eyes charged at her and she quickly threw one of the pebbles on the ground. She disappeared and re-appeared at the bank of the second river. She walked towards the river and repeated the words she said at the first river and the river parted for her to walk through.

When Aku arrived at the third river, she encountered a beautiful woman with very long, tangled hair. The woman asked Aku to help her detangled her hair and Aku obliged. She set to work but the hair was too matted to detangle. A voice told her to play the bamboo flute and she obeyed. The beautiful woman began to dance to the sweet melody of the music and her tangled long hair began to detangle itself. When all her hairs were untangled, the beautiful woman stopped dancing. She thanked Aku and gave her a cowry and a strand from her hair, saying,

"Present this cowry and strand of my hair to the guard at the entrance where the magic clay pot is kept. He will tell you what to do. Go well my child."

Aku walked to the third river and repeated the words she used in crossing the first and second rivers, and the river parted for her to walk to the other side. She saw the tree that the two-headed demon told her about. She went to it and plucked three ripe fruits from it. She ate the fruits and felt her strength renewed.

Aku got to the entrance where the magic clay pot was kept and was stopped by the guards there.

"Where are you going to? And who authorized you to come to the land of the dead?"

"I am Aku and I came to collect the magic clay pot, which will be used to heal my village crown prince from a strange illness," she replied.

She then presented the cowry and the strand of the beautiful woman's hair to them. The guard accepted it and gave her a long veil saying,

"Cover your face with this veil and also use the edge of the veil to pick up the magic clay pot."

Aku thanked them and did as she was instructed. She collected the small magic clay pot and put it in her goatskin bag. On her way home, she saw a mango tree with beautiful ripe mangoes on it. The forces surrounding the tree lured her to pluck a mango and eat from it. As soon as she finished eating the mango, she fell into a deep sleep beside the tree.

Meanwhile, back at the village, King Egbe, Ulo and the Chief Priest became worried because Aku did not return at the expected time and the Chief Priest had lost track of her whereabouts. Prince Ike's health had gotten so bad that he was only expected to live for four more days. Ulo went to the Chief Priest seeking solutions on how to bring back her daughter from the land of the dead but the Chief Priest told her,

"The gods are still silent about her whereabouts but do not be afraid, woman, Aku will return safely. The gods of our land will not fail us."

Ulo went home crying bitterly and calling on the gods to pity her and bring back her daughter safely to her.

Back in the land of the dead, Aku dreamt of her mother crying and calling her to come home to her. She went to comfort her then she woke up from the deep sleep. At first she was confused and could not recognize where she was. Then she remembered that she was still in the land of the dead. Not knowing what to do and how to get home, she brought out the bamboo flute and started playing it. The sweet melody from the flute attracted seven spirits to the spot where she was and they started dancing to the music. They danced and danced and danced until she stopped playing the flute.

"Please play it again for us, we will reward you with whatever you ask for," they said.

Again, Aku began to play the flute and they resume their dancing. When they were satisfied, they told Aku to name her prize and she said,

"I want to go home to my mother and little brother, please."

They gave her an egg, instructing her to break it at the middle of four roads. She accepted the egg from them and thanked them for their generosity. When she got to the middle of four pathways, she broke the egg as instructed and she immediately disappeared and appeared at the boundary between the living and the dead.

Suddenly, the magic clay pot in her goatskin bag began to rattle. She brought it out and the clay pot revealed to her that Prince Ike was gasping for air. She immediately put the magic clay pot back into her goatskin bag and started running to the palace. As she got close, a voice told her to stop by the river and fetch water from the river with the magic clay pot. Aku obeyed. As she dipped the magic clay pot into the river, the river became purified by the touch of the magic clay pot. She fetched the water and proceeded to the palace.

When she arrived at the palace, the Chief Priest welcomed her and instructed everyone to let her do what she needed to do. She went straight to Prince Ike's room where he was still struggling to breathe and gave him the water from the magic clay pot. Immediately, the fever ravaging the Prince's body stopped. The Chief Priest gave Aku a bucket of cleansing water to bathe with and cleanse herself from the stench of the dead. After the cleansing bath, Aku narrated her ordeals in the land of the dead to the King and everyone present. She told them that it was the tears of her mother that woke her up from the deep sleep the evil mango fruit inflicted on her. Her mother was very happy; she hugged Aku and thanked the gods of the land for bringing her daughter back to her safely. King Egbe declared a four-day feast in the village in honour of the return of Aku from the land of the dead and the recovery of his son's health. He mandated Aku's uncles to return all the properties they took from Ulo and also to vacate Aku's father's house. Aku, her mother and little brother returned to their home with lots of livestock, foodstuffs and money given to them by the King.

Three days later, Prince Ike visited Aku, her mother and little brother in their house. He thanked Aku for the ordeals she went through in the land of the dead to restore his health.

"Aku, you are a very beautiful girl with a kind heart. Will you marry me and rule our village by my side?"

Aku and her mother were very excited by his proposal and she accepted the offer. King Egbe was very happy that it was Aku that his son chose as wife. He blessed them and they lived happily for many years.

Our Dream Changed The Entire Story

By Brian Ochieng
A Story From Kenya

It was seven o'clock in the morning and the tranquility that filled the air kept Ochieng in his bed. He yawned several times and stood up to stretch beside his bed. The birds seemed to welcome the rising sun with their melodious songs. Odhiambo, Ochieng's elder brother, was still sleeping and could be heard snoring heavily. Ochieng left the house and found his stepmother, Ayoo, sitting with her friends under a jacaranda tree, chatting and laughing irritatingly as if they owned the morning and no one was allowed to sleep if they were awake. Ochieng just smiled because he hoped for a good day and believed that yesterday is but a dream, and tomorrow a vision.

While Ochieng was still lost in thought, he heard an ululation from the neighborhood. They all ran towards it to find out what was happening in the neighboring home of the chief of the clan called *Ruoth Mugo*, or King Mugo. People were dancing to the Luo cultural songs as some played instruments like *nyatiti* (bowl yoke lute), *orutu* (harp), *abu*, and *bul* (drum). This was done in preparation for the delivery of the chief's wife, *Nyar Kamagambo*. Older women and midwives, commonly referred to as *nyamrerwa*, assisted *Nyar Kamagambo* through her pregnancy and, on this fateful day, her childbirth.

Moods changed and whispers spread as the people found out that the chief's wife had given birth to twins. It was believed that twins were a result of evil spirits, which the Luo usually treated with utmost concern, as it required taboos on the part of the *Ruoth* and his family. People were quiet as it was also believed that if one used foul language during that period, the burden of giving birth to twins would be passed on to the next generation. *Dala Ruoth*, or the house of the king, was in loud, suffocating silence as a ritual was performed immediately to communicate with the ancestors to ask for their forgiveness. A black sheep and a hen, which were associated with evil because of their black color, were slaughtered and their blood poured on the ground for the ancestors as a sign of asking for forgiveness. This ritual was spearheaded by the *jodongo*, or elder, who used a flywhisk to send away *juok*, or witchcraft. People departed to their various homes and the mood was somber.

Ochieng was hungry and decided to walk into the *jikon*, or kitchen, to find something to prepare for breakfast since his cold-hearted step-mother never bothered to cook anything for them unless their father, Omori, was there. Even then she would only prepare some *ugali* and black tea without sugar. Food was a luxury in this family and it was like *hawi*, or luck, from God whenever they had something to eat on a single day, and it was rare for them to get more than one meal a day. Their biological mother, Mary, had been possessed by evil spirits, called *juogi* in the Luo tradition, and was quite dangerous. When they attacked her, she would turn wild and harm people around her unintentionally, as well as hurt herself by piercing her body using pebbles, causing her a lot of unbearable pain. At times, she ran out of the house stripping herself naked. The women in the neighborhood would run after her with *sukas* to cover her nakedness before people could see her. She would scream and speak in tongues that no one could interpret.

On many occasions, Mary was isolated to prevent her from hurting other people. This led to Ochieng and Odhiambo being brought up by their stepmother. Their father was polygamous and had two wives, Ayoo the first wife, and their mother Mary. Unfortunately for Ayoo, she was barren. She realized that her husband did not love her as much as he did Mary and she decided to fake a pregnancy when he was on a business trip. She paid a midwife in the village to tell a woman who just gave birth that her baby was stillborn. Ayoo took the baby and named her Liza. The Luo regarded having children as a form of wealth; thus many men were polygamous in order to have many children and gain respect in the community. Being polygamous had benefited Omori for he was highly regarded in the community and was able to become an elder.

Ochieng left the house and walked past the compound to go look for some guavas to ease his hunger. In the bushes, he found guavas, which they called *mapera*, mango, which was *maembe*, and some oxalis plant, which they referred to as *awayo*. This was to ease his hunger before he went to the great lake. Ochieng and his brother would boil the fruit in *agulu*, or a pot, for seven minutes or so until it was tender. They would then add salt and serve it in *aguata*, or a calabash cup. Occasionally, they would add an oxalis bloom for better nutrition and color enhancement. After eating this concoction, they had enough energy to go to *Nam Lolwe*, commonly known as Lake Victoria, which was walking distance from their home, to catch *ngege,* or tilapia.

Their catch was often unpredictable and many were the times they would go back home with nothing at all, and the looks on their faces would show the disappointment they felt deep within them. This time around, however, they had luck. Odhiambo placed a bucket made from sisal tied with *modhno*, or grass, inside the water. He then tied about three to four strings to a long stick and immersed it into the water. As the fish rushed into the trap, he pulled it out of the water, catching the fish and at the same time tried to use a sharpened twig to spear the fish. When they pulled out the trap, there was a big *ngege* in it, which was a blessing and would be shared with every member of the family. This was the level of poverty in this community where putting food on the table was a real struggle.

Odhiambo and Ochieng were the sole providers of the family since their stepmother did not bother to go out to look for food. She considered them her stepsons and she was jealous of Mary because she herself never bore any child especially a boy child. It was said in their village of *Kamrimbo* that Ayoo was a woman who liked visiting the *ajuoga*, or witch. When her husband married Mary after realizing Ayoo was barren, she was very reluctant to welcome Mary to the family and became very cold and hostile towards her. She felt left out and unloved when her husband began showing more love and attention to Mary who was able to bear children. Marriage without lovemaking brings sad consequences and sorrows. Ayoo visited the *ajuoga* and had a spell cast on Mary, which was how Mary became possessed by *juogi* that made her lose her mind and clouded almost all her memory as well as her thoughts.

A daily routine for Odhiambo and his brother was to wake up and go out to find something that they could eat to sustain them. They had adapted to survival and food was never for satisfaction but for sustenance. On their way to look for food in the morning, they would meet children dressed in their neat uniforms walking to school, talking in a strange language that neither of them could understand. The simple English that those children were speaking fascinated the brothers and they would look at the children walking down the road to school with admiration until they disappeared around a bend on the road. Odhiambo turned to Ochieng and stared at him from toe to head and back and Ochieng did the same. They noticed a big difference between themselves and those children who looked neat, smart and elegant as opposed to them who wore dirty, torn clothers, or *omethe*. Their clothes were so torn that Odhiambo's belly was not totally covered and you could see Ochieng's buttocks from behind.

The boys were forced to drop out of school when their mother fell sick and Ayoo was not willing to pay their fees because they were a burden to her. The brothers had to bear with the situation because at the end of the day it was about how much you can bear, and how much you can endure. Odhiambo and the brother had a dream of one day being great people in their society and change their story into one of a lifestyle of abundance.

Their ill mother's brother, Omollo, who they referred to as *nera*, paid them a visit and brought them some food to eat and new clothes. He was able to see the suffering the boys were undergoing just by the way they would scramble for food even though there was enough for everyone in the family. There was evidence of malnourishment in the boys and on their faces. Their uncle really pitied them for what they were going through despite being such innocent souls. You would not be able to guess what the boys were going through, and from their smile, you would think all was well but this was clearly not the case.

There is a sweet innocence in being human and not having to be just happy or just sad in the nature of being able to be both broken and whole at the same time.

When their uncle was leaving, he decided to take Ochieng, the younger boy, with him for a visit to his place just for one day and promised to bring him back in the following day. He was not able to take both of them with him because he had an *ndiga*, a bicycle, and he was only able to carry one passenger. He chose the little boy and not the elder brother because he wanted to question him about what had been going on and if they had been attending school. He knew that Ochieng would be honest unlike Odhiambo who would choose to hide the truth to make their stay at their stepmother's house peaceful. On several occasions, they had been threatened with being sent away if they told their father or anyone else that they were no longer going to school. Ayoo did not know that to threaten the brave with death is like promising water to a duck. Ochieng believed that if a man threatens you, sleep at night; if it is by a woman, then stay awake.

Ochieng told his uncle about everything that was going on including their being mistreated and forced to drop out of school to look for food for the family while their half-sister Liza was attending a nearby school in their village. Omollo decided to take both boys with him so that they could attend school. The following day, instead of taking Ochieng back home, he asked Ayoo to let both boys stay with him for some time. She could not refuse because Omollo was their uncle, so Odhiambo joined his brother at their uncle's place. They were having good time together and the smiles on their faces were more genuine. This made their *nera* happy and he arranged for the boys to go to school. He let their father know by sending him a message via the Post and after a few days, the father replied giving his appreciation to Omollo for taking up the responsibility, which was supposed to be his own obligation. This reminded Omori of the words of John F Kennedy, a former president of the United

States of America, who once said,

"As we express our gratitude, we must never forget that the highest appreciation is not to utter words but to live by them."

Omollo fully took over the responsibility to take the boys to school. The boys were doing their best in school and from their teachers came good comments. The boys were determined in their work and their teachers were surprised by how fast they were adapting and catching up with the rest. At the end of the term, the boys had a stunning performance in their academic work. Their teachers and their uncle were happy with their progress despite them being away from school for a long period. The brothers were determined, self-disciplined, humble and loyal, and their teachers said that was going to add up to their success and nothing was going to deter them from achieving their dreams.

Ochieng often remembered the good times he used to spend with his *dani*, or grandmother, who was known as *Nyar Asembo*. She used to call them when they returned from the *puodho* , or garden, and tell them the story of two friends, *Apuoyo* and *Ondiegi,* who lived a long time ago. In the *siwidhe, Nyar Asembo* presided over the story telling and verbal games. Riddles took the form of competitive exchange where winners were rewarded by play *nyombo,* or play marriage, to the girls. There would be friendly arguments that would erupt over the interpretation of riddles, which made it even more interesting as it challenged every child to think for the reason for their answer. Their grandmother used to teach them about their traditions and how their ancestors communicated with the living to pass either a message or a warning to the community. They would send dreams to the living, to children or adults, and it was recommended that any strange dreams be reported to *Jaduong Gweng*, or Elder Gweng, for interpretation. There were good spirits as well as evil spirits which caused trouble in the community and were a result of bad send-off of some ancestors, or ancestors who were not pleased with things the living were doing.

A few days later, Ochieng had a dream and he remembered what his grandmother used to tell them when she was still alive. He went to an old man called *Jaduong Odero* who was living in a nearby homestead. After he shared the dream with him, the old man stood holding his *arungu*, or knobkerry, while facing the rising sun. Ochieng could not understand why but after a short while, *Jaduong Odero* told Ochieng to follow him as he led the way back to Omori's home. The whole family was seated outside, under the tree. He pointed directly at Omori's wife, Ayoo, and told her to confess her sins before the ancestor's wrath was cast onto the whole community. Ayoo, in fear, confessed how she had visited the *ajuoga* in order to cast a spell on her *nyieke*, or co-wife, Mary, because she had *nyiego*, or jealousy, that their husband loved her more and she always tried to have her sent away although she never succeeded. She also confessed to denying Ochieng and Odhiambo a chance to go to school and instead using them to fetch food for the family without their father's consent. *Jaduong Gweng* called a meeting to discuss Ayoo's behavior. Being the first wife allowed her to escape punishment though she was told to seek forgiveness from whomever she mistreated. According to the interpreted dream, it was possible for Mary to be cured as the ancestors regarded her as an innocent being. The *jodongo* decided that a ritual had to be performed to cast out the *juogi* from Mary to save her and bring her back to normal.

The ceremony began the following day at dawn. Mary was brought in and everyone was present. During *miend*, or dance, *juogi* and *mwadzindika* dance, the dancers dramatized the activities of the healing process. The cleanser moved to the possessed and poured water on her head, with the dance becoming more provoking and involving. The dance climax, known as *yiengo*, or shake, *juogi*, was one of awe, wonder and admiration at the techniques of drummers. The Luos believed that *juogi* was afraid of *min bul*, or the huge drum. Thus it did not take long for Mary to recover fully after that. Everybody rejoiced and, afterwards, Ayoo asked her for forgiveness. Mary did not find it hard to forgive her. The whole community came together and held a ceremony.

Ochieng and his brother were also successful in their academics and were able to find employment after graduation. Ochieng became the Manager of Seeds Limited Company while Odhiambo became the Head of the Research Institutes of Agriculture. They both had a good standard of living and were able to provide for themselves, as well as give back to the community by paying school fees to the less fortunate children and supporting needy families. Omori's family was now a happy home. The family ate dinner together, after which Ochieng would recite a word of prayer before everyone retired to bed. They all went to sleep with a smile on their faces.

The Decision

Melinda Barthel
A story from Zambia

As was custom in my tribe, the women had gone to draw water before the sun had begun to kiss the earth with its warmth. And I, even though the daughter of the chief of the Kaonde people, had to go with them. I had to learn the ways of our people, our women, just as all the other girls. I knew no other way so I had no cause to complain. It had been so since the time of our ancestors, and as far as I could think it would remain forever so. How wrong I was. How the gods must have laughed at my naive thinking. But since I did not know it, I reveled in the pleasure of being young and alive, in the changing voices of the forest as we glided through it, of the gentle singing of the older girls as we walked in single file over the well-known path. My heart leaped so within me and I thought surely it would fall out for joy.

"How you beam, Kutemwa!" exclaimed my best friend as she turning in that moment caught a look at my face. "What thoughts dance through that noble head of yours, pray do tell."

"And how curious you are, Lubuto. Beware of the hunter; curious creatures fall into his trap. And then it is too late."

"What nonsense you speak. What do you know of hunting? But if you do not spit out the words they will choke you as surely as the sun will rise tomorrow."

But how could I tell her of things I could not express myself. My heart spoke a language that words could not utter. She broke into my thoughts by saying,

"If I did not know better I would think the hunter had caught your heart in his trap."

"Now you are the one who spews out nonsense!" I answered, a bit too strongly perhaps. "What use do I have for one when I have you?" That set her off into fits of laughter and I couldn't help but add the melody of mine to hers.

"Just wait and see." she murmured. I pretended not to hear her and she smiled. I went back to my thoughts.

We arrived finally at the banks of the Zambezi. It looked so deceptively beautiful, but we all knew that danger lurked beneath its waters. Just in the rainy season, it had claimed the child of one of the village women. She still mourned his passing even though many full moons had come and gone. He had been a sweet child. My heart had gone out to her. So while one of us kept a look out for crocodiles and hippos, the others bathed.

Our calabashes full, we turned back towards home. Gone was the spring in my step. Whenever we stepped out of the shadows of the trees, the sun blazed unmercifully down on us. Perhaps we had delayed too long. As if reading my thoughts, the steps of the other women quickened as did their song. Without warning, I slipped on a stone that had been loosened by the many anxious feet that had gone before. I came tumbling down as ungracefully as a tree that had been felled. I lay stunned for a moment, not realizing what had happened.

"Kutemwa, are you alright?" chorused many anxious voices. I did not realize what fear was coursing through their veins until I managed to utter a breathless "yes." I read relief on their faces but could not really understand why.

" I'm fine" I said, "but my water pot?"

"It survived, the gods be praised," answered one, " but you will have to carry it empty today."

I didn't really mind actually. Each step had been harder to take than the previous with the calabash on my head. Lubuto volunteered to remain behind and walk at a slower pace with me until I had recovered. We were not too far from the village so the other women readily agreed and went on ahead. On reaching a shady glen, I asked Lubuto if we could rest for a bit. She agreed and we sat on a fallen tree, talking quietly between ourselves. Suddenly she spotted some mushrooms in the distance and decided to go pick them. She thought it would justify our being late if we had something to show for it. I excused myself and she didn't argue.

How long I sat I do not know but suddenly I realized I was not alone anymore. My first thought was to scream in panic and bring Lubuto back to my side. But I was the daughter of a chief; I would not disgrace my father's name by behaving like a coward.

"Show yourself, whoever you are." I said authoritatively, or at least I hoped so.

He appeared. The most handsome of boys I had ever seen, but his most drawing features were his eyes. How he sparkled, like the lights of a thousand stars. Forgotten was our tradition of women never looking men in the face, and our eyes locked for what seemed like an eternity. I felt my heart begin to stir inside me and I was afraid. I lowered my eyes and could not look at him again.

He spoke. His voice was like music but I did not understand a word he said. He stopped. He spoke again. This time in my mother tongue though it sounded strange in his mouth. His name was Wana of the Lunda tribe. He had been in pursuit of an impala and had been led far from his normal hunting grounds. I neither spoke nor looked at him. He hesitated when he noticed that I was giving no response to him.

"Do you understand what I am saying?" he asked, "I don't know any Luvale, just Kaonde and Lunda"

I nodded. A quick glance at his face through my eyelashes showed me his relief and a smile tugged at my face.

"You laugh at me," he said. Then I did laugh and so did he. It was melody to my ears. It made my stomach quiver. In that moment Lubuto joined us, ready for battle like a mother leopard.

"It's alright," I told her. "He was only asking for directions."

She scolded me in a fierce whisper about acting like a chicken with its head cut off and practically dragged me away from him. I threw a glance over my shoulder and he winked at me and smiled. Then he was gone. Lubuto scolded me all the way home but I never heard a word she said. Wana may have failed to catch the impala, but he had captured my heart.

Every time we walked in the forest, to draw water, or to gather fruit or mushrooms, my heart and my eyes searched for him, but it would be many sunrises and sunsets before I would see him again.

One day we went to gather a root called chikanda. It was washed, sliced dried and then pounded into a fine powder. It was then cooked with groundnuts that had also been pounded to a fine powder. Lastly, water mixed with ashes and sieved of all particles was added making it into a solid. The resulting cake was delicious. Some people added chilli to give it a kick but I preferred the mild version. We were spread out over a wild area when I heard a bird call that did not quite sound like bird call. It was him. Every fibre of my being knew it. Trying to keep my voice steady, I called out to Lubuto.

"I'm going a little way in the forest to relieve myself."

"Make sure you check carefully before you squat. We don't want any red ants thinking you are the meal do we?"

We both laughed. But it had happened once to an unfortunate man in our village and songs were sang about the incident for many moons afterwards. He had stopped to relieve himself but so intently that he didn't realize that red ants where crossing his path until they first began to bite him.

My heart had longed for his nearness for too long and I threw caution to the wind. Our eyes met and held.

"You never told me you name," he said.

"Kutemwa."

"Kukena," he said. "The foolish is made wiser."

I couldn't follow his murmuring and I guess he saw it from my face.

"That is your name in my mother tongue," he explained, "Kukena."

When he said my name, it sounded like the tumbling of a stream.

"I have had many sleepless nights because of you, 'Love of Life.' I did not know how much longer I could have held out without seeing you again. Strange, so strange," he said more to himself than to me.

It pleased me to no end to know that I had not left his thoughts. It was a delightful thought, making me smile.

"You always seem to laugh at me," he said.

"And you always say that," I said. We almost laughed but caught ourselves. I could hear Lubuto's anxious voice calling for me.

"I must go," I said.

"I must see you again," he replied.

"Tomorrow, we will go to catch crabs by the Zambezi banks where the hippos normally cross. Be there and I will see if I can come to you."

"Kutemwa!"

"I'm coming, Lubuto, I'm coming."

He touched my hand briefly smiled and was gone as silently as the shadows. He must be an excellent hunter, I thought. My other hand wandered to where his had rested and I smiled dreamily. So began our love. I became cunning in slipping away for short moments from the other women whenever I heard his bird call. Not even Lubuto suspected anything. Our love was the strongest love that ever was. Nothing and no one could tear us apart. Here, again, I would be proved naive in my thinking.

The gods would have been kinder if they had not sent the white man into my life. But my father was the chief and, as was custom, I had to show hospitality to them. On the day they arrived, we watched in fascination. How long they must have hidden from the sun to become so pale. There were two of them and an interpreter who spoke our mother tongue. Their speech sounded in our ears like a child learning to talk, but he could understand them, it seemed. They showed us many wonderful things: paper that could sing, water that smelled like a thousand roses, but my favorite was something they called a mirror. Of course I had seen my reflection many times in the river but since it was ever alive my reflection always followed its movements. But in the mirror my image stood before me in such clarity it took my breath away. I was quite pleased at the features that stared back at me. At least I had inherited some of my mother's beauty.

Then they spoke of a God. He seemed to have made the whole world and its people. But we worshiped our ancestors and many others: the gods of the rain, the harvest, war, and love. Why, since I was a child, I had learned which god was responsible for what affairs of the world and how we were not to displease them. In case we did, we pacified them with drinks and offering. These people talked about this God coming to earth as a child and growing and dying and then coming back to life. We listened politely as was our custom with visitors but no one took them seriously.

I continued my secret meetings with Wana and related to him all that the missionaries told us. He seemed fascinated and I was too foolish to realize where the fascination was leading. If only someone had caused my tongue to hang to the roof of my mouth. But propelled by love, I faithfully related every conversation almost word for word.

With the passing of days, they began to pick up some words from our tongue. Because they sounded so funny whenever they spoke it, every once in a while just for our amusement we would gather round them and make them speak the little they knew. The children would laugh until their bellies ached, but after our fun they insisted that we listen to them. So we did. It did seem like a fair exchange to us; besides it gave me more to relate to Wana whose curiosity seemed as endless as the savanna.

Lubuto and I took them around to show them the forest and the source of the Zambezi in the Kalena hills. We were the few who could be spared from the daily chores of village life. Apart from their endless chatter about their God, the excursions were wonderful, especially for meeting up with Wana. For that I would have liked them to stay longer. They also taught me how to write my name. It was strange to see the squiggles in the sand that were supposed to be my name, but they eventually registered on my brain and began to make sense.

The missionaries left. Many moons passed and like an unborn baby we forgot about them. But one day they were brought painfully to my remembrance. Wana, the heartbeat of my life, embraced this new God. He who was heir to the throne of the Lundas. He would no longer do the daily sacrificial rituals or ancestral worship required of him as the heir. In so doing, he ignited the anger of his father the chief, and the elders of the tribe. They carried out an investigation and found out the missionaries had stayed in our village. A meeting between the chiefs and elders of both tribes were held in my village. The day dawned clear and blue with endless sky as far as the eye could see. Who could have thought that such a day would bring black clouds of anger, disappointment and heartache our way.

71

They gathered under the mango tree which provided the most shelter from the already scorching sun, but did nothing against the scorching words that were soon to follow. The women and children formed the outer circle, the men the inner one. I trembled at my mother's knee and she gave me a reassuring smile. If only she knew, I thought, and another shiver shook me.

Angry words and accusations flew across the floor. My heart beat terrified within me like a bird caught in a trap. Wana's father accused mine of bewitching his son so that his chiefdom would be without an heir. My father denied ever having seen Wana at all. He said it was true that he had given the missionaries sanctuary in his village, but they had left with their strange tales of another God with them.

"No one in my village believed their idle tales. And if your son believed them, then you did not raise him well."

"Ask your daughter," he spat out.

I cringed with fear. My father's face which was usually so love-filled looked like that of an angry stranger as he turned to me.

"Kutemwa!"

"Mwane," I barely managed to whisper.

"Do you know this boy?"

" Ya, Tata," our word for father.

"How long?"

"Since before the missionaries came."

My father looked questioningly at my mother. She raised helpless hands. Lubuto's mouth fell open. I stared at the ground as hard as I could hoping that it would give me refuge. Then Wana stood up and began to talk. His words made my stomach churn with fear.

"I love your daughter."

There was an angry buzz of voices and one or two elders spat into the dust as a sign of their disapproval at his boldness, but he continued.

"She told me what the missionaries had said and suddenly my eyes and my heart was opened to the truth. The decision was my own. No one and nothing forced me to it. But I cannot deny what my heart has come to believe. I wish your hearts would be opened too, that you would know what a burden was lifted off of me when I met this God. My heart yearns to know more about him. And even today I will set off after the missionaries so that I can learn more about this God. Forgive me, father. Forgive me, Kukena."

The shock that hung in the air at this final statement could be cut with an axe. My heart grew cold as it finally dawned on me what his words meant for me.

"No, Wana," I heard myself crying, "Don't go! My song, my heart, my breath."

My mother tried to quieten me. But as I saw him, tall and proud, turn his back on his people, on our love, to follow a God I had told him about, I became hysterical. With outstretched arms, I willed him back and as if sensing it, he looked at me, no smile, no wink, long and hard and walked off.

I wept, till my eyes were swollen shut and I couldn't see, till my voice was just a hoarse whisper in my throat. Our love had been strong, but his love for the white man's God proved stronger and they took from me my love, my song, my breath and my childhood. I became a woman. Though our tribes are known as cousin tribes, it would be many full moons before the breach caused by Wana's leaving would begin to mend. My heart needed longer. He took it with him when he left.

The Adventure

By Tanyi Nkongho
A story from Cameroon

Once, a group of seven students from the city came for vacation to their village called *Nkewa*. They had left the village setting when they were in primary school and only visited the village again when they were at university. With time away from the village, they missed out on many activities they would normally have participated in like bathing in the stream, community firewood fetching, dance competitions, and watching the sunset in the evenings since the village is located in the mountains.

With all the excitement burning within them over their return and seeing their old friends, loved ones and much more, they made sure they engaged in all the activities they had missed out on, and chitchatted with old friends to make up for lost time.

After all the excitement had died down, these students decided to organize something even more interesting like going for an adventure in the forest, not knowing that the forest in question was a forbidden forest.

The forest named *Ekuh* is a dangerous forest with a shrine, and people believed to have practiced magic and witchcraft in the village are buried in this shrine. Each time a burial has to be performed, a ritual which involves human sacrifice is done before anyone steps into the forbidden forest, otherwise everyone risks not leaving the forest alive. Unfortunately, these aspiring adventurers weren't aware of the history surrounding this forest and they didn't seek advice from their parents or friends. This same forest is also known as the forest where their gods duel.

This same forest is tied to a mystery of a lost prince who happens to be the only son of the dead king of Nkewa. The gods of the land had held him captive for refusal to succeed his father after his death. The prince was a Christian and believed in God's words. He didn't want to engage in barbaric bloodshed and unholy practices surrounding a king and the so-called cleansing of the land. However, he wasn't very spiritual; that is, he was more like an average believer.

The prince had been tied in the shrine for months and he prayed for God to help him so that he could be set free. But the only way for him to be free was for the gods to find someone else worthy enough to be king. Otherwise he would be bound to remain there and pay the price of no liberty.

On a Friday evening, the students packed food, water, weapons and a few items of emergency clothing, thinking they were going for a harmless and exciting discovery, not knowing that was the beginning of the worst experience of their lives. Five of them, 3 girls and 2 boys, left very early the following morning at

6:00 am for the journey, while 2 stayed back as they weren't ready for such a journey due to schools resuming in a fortnight.

The journey started on an exciting note and the students were thrilled in the beginning as they talked, ate, hunted, made fun of each other, and laughed with great delight. It went well until they found themselves in the interior of a forest which was very quiet, dark and scary with only the sounds of wild birds and trees. They couldn't retrace their steps so they exclaimed, "Where are we?" They were confused and baffled on what to do next or how to proceed with the journey or even how to get back. All excitement immediately turned sour with everyone looking at each other with fearful eyes. The ladies were shivering already and wished they had also stayed back, but unfortunately, they didn't know how to get back.

The clouds had covered the sky and it became dark. They used their touch light to look for a comfortable place to camp for the night. They gathered some wood and lit a fire to scare wild animals and warm themselves up. They couldn't even talk comfortably but rather they whispered to each other.

With their presence disturbing the forest of the gods, there was a signal in the shrine indicating the presence of mortals. The gods exhibited their powers in their territory and sealed all exit paths of the forest, making sure none of them would escape.

When the students were fast asleep, a scary creature which cannot be adequately described with words appeared where they camped and laughed so loudly that they woke up and started running. In the ensuing confusion, everyone ran in different directions and thus they got separated. They ran all night till morning broke. As they were running, some of them lost their bags containing everything they carried, but others at least retained their water. None of them could find their way out of the forest.

By noon the next day, another creature appeared to each of them, and again they ran. Fortunately, they ran into each other but one of the girls wasn't among them. They pondered where she could be and what might have happened to her. They searched for her until nightfall to no avail. It was the second night and they camped again. While they were still contemplating their situation, they heard a loud voice saying,

"You all shall die." He continued, "You can't leave this forest alive, just like your friend."

At that point they knew they were in a terrible situation, and they realized their friend was dead. They wept and cried out for help but they couldn't be helped, and it seemed like there was danger everywhere.

They left and camped elsewhere, and spent the night sobbing and praying for a way out. The next morning, they continued moving and looking for a way to leave the forest, but the more they tried, the further they got into the forest. They went about for days moving in circles but they with no success. Their initial plan was a three-day adventure, but it had been a week already in the forest and they had lost all their strength due to hunger. They could barely walk or talk, and were already giving up on life because they knew their end was death. They finally camped at a spot and stopped trying to leave the forest despite the school start date fast approaching.

The parents became worried and started inquiring where their children were. The students didn't tell their parents exactly where they planned to go because they didn't want to be stopped by their parents. On the other hand, the two friends that didn't go along were also as worried and scared for their friends since they weren't back yet. The friends were questioned and they had to let the cat out of the bag. Their parents were shocked, depressed and confused on what action to take because they knew that the consequence of trespassing in the forest was death. Under normal circumstances, the gods would use them as sacrifices for breaking the rules. Family members and friends could only cry with and console the families, but they hoped for a miracle.

The information had gone viral in the local community and got to the ears of a man called Amerane. This man had spiritual abilities to see things beyond the mortals. He was consulted to find out if the students were still alive or dead. He confirmed they were alive but also mentioned that the gods had sealed all exit routes. He continued, "Unfortunately, they all can't make it out of the forest alive because I didn't see one person," and he couldn't figure out who in particular was already dead. He said for the gods to unseal the exit paths, more blood must be shed, or they could let the gods decide their fate. They thought it unreasonable to shed a human's blood to save another so they decided to go with the second option while hoping the gods would show mercy.

In the forest, the gods came to the students as they slept and provided them with some vegetables and water so they could regain their strength. One rule of the gods is that they don't feed on unhealthy beings. The students woke up and found the food. With the great hunger and thirst they felt, they didn't hesitate to consume the food and water, not caring how they got there. As they finished, they were strong again and wished they never came to the forest to begin with. They thought of school starting which was in five days and shed tears bitterly.

They stood up and looked around to see if they could find a way out but a strong force was compelling them to move towards the west where lay the secret shrine. From a distance, they saw an image like a cave that seemed like an outlet, but they didn't know it was the path that led to the shrine of *Ekuh*. They got closer and decided to go through the cave but ended up at the entrance of the shrine. They stared at each other and were astounded. They heard the voice of someone crying from inside for help in their language and they rushed to help out but later withdrew and decided that two persons would go first.

As the two people stepped forth to check who was crying, they were startled as they saw an exhausted man, who was the prince, tied to a tree. As they untied him, the gods struck the two of them while the prince ran out screaming with tears flowing down his cheeks. He met the two standing outside, shouted and ran. He had in his possession a tiny magic broom which when hit against a tree, could open all sealed roads. As they followed him, he did just that and they finally had a path that led them out of the circle of the gods.

The gods couldn't kill the prince because he had royal blood but for him to be set free, two people were sacrificed at the spot. In the end, just two of the students returned home, a man and a lady, alongside the prince. There was happiness for the prince's return but sadness for the lost souls. It's unfortunate the students lost their lives but it was a disguised answered prayer for the prince. A mourning ceremony was organized by the prince and everyone was expected to take part for three days with no engagement in farming or other economic activities. After the mourning ceremony, the students returned to school and the prince transferred the chieftaincy rights to a different family.

Michael Mazukulu, The Zimbabwean Struggle

By Khutso Modika Eron

A Story from Zimbabwe

Sloppy cheeks of a miserable, 25 year old foreigner. The struggle in our country was too much. The jobs were not there and that education system was just a trap. It was so irrelevant to have those qualifications. Our president was just a clown with promises. Each day it was him promising us heaven and earth, but behind his speeches we all knew that it was just a trap to lure us into voting more for him so that he could continue to bring more suffering into our lives.

My name is Michael Mazukulu, a Zimbabwean citizen. The father of three, two daughters and one son. Elizabeth Mazukulu and Rose Mazukulu are my daughters, and Jack Mazukulu is my son. I wish I had a perfect empire to leave them with, but I feel less of a man for starving them this much. My wife Loraine Mazukulu, the mother of my children, the exquisite flower in my garden. She has been very supportive since day one. The Mazukulu family; we are only five in total in a two-room hut with wrinkled walls.

But as the man of the family, it is a must to wake up and find a way to provide food for your wife and kids. I hated each and every moment I had to open my eyes early mornings with nothing but a hungry stomach. The looks you receive from your hungry wife and kids when you unemployed are so heartbreaking. The looks of hunger, the looks of "we are tired of struggle" from their eyes ate me alive every time I had to gaze back at them. Each morning I had to wake up and prepare my fishing stick, and a can full of worms, then head straight to the nearby river.

It is hard being the man of the family with dry pockets, seeing the lips of your wife and children slowly drying because of hunger. The jobs were not there. I was retrenched from an oil-making factory. This is the reason I am unemployed right now and still have to watch my wife and kids suffer every day. My monthly salary from the factory was 1,000 Zimbabwean dollars. With it, I was able to pay monthly school fees for my children, buy food and also give my wife some to save, but with this retrenchment thing, our savings vanished. And hunger keeps knocking so aggressively on our door.

The factory shut down due to relocation reasons that left Jason

Gymblowski without any other option but to retrench his staff. Jason Gymblowski was the oil factory owner. His decision became a death sentence to some of us as the husbands in our households. He killed us big time as I was forced to watch my kids kicked out of school due to months of unpaid school fees. How hypocritical of our government system, paying school fees for your children and still watch them failing to find a job; the unemployment rate was increasing rapidly every year. But as a parent, you can't allow your kids to sit while others are going to school. That will only make you look like a man who doesn't care about his kids and their education. Even if the education system was becoming very clear to my perspective that is was nothing but a trap of unemployment, the choice wasn't there at all but to do what the other parents were doing. Taking them to school as well, it was so heartwarming seeing their marks so high and beautiful. But with this retrenchment going, they also had to suffer.

Sometimes I remember my father's words, "Don't ever allow your wife and kids to suffer while you still alive."

Jeffrey Mazukulu was his name. Unfortunately he was captured by the American army in 1980. I wonder what they did to him, turned him into a slave maybe? Or even worse, killed him? Truth is we will never know. He only told us to look after our mother and never bother ourselves to cry for him, but our mother also died because of a heart disease two years ago. Gabriel Mazukulu, the only brother I have, my father loved him so much. I remember when we were still young, my father would come home from work and start telling us stories that,

"As a man, it is a must to go against a dragon in order to make sure that your family does not suffer from hunger."

A dragon? Gabriel and I just stood there so dumbfounded, wondering what he could be talking about.

But what was he really talking about? Like are we supposed to hunt dragons, kill them and eat them with our families? Sometimes we thought maybe he was losing it because this wasn't even the century of dragons. What was he really talking about? He never stopped but kept on going,

"As a man you have to make sure that your wife and children does not suffer from hunger. If possible fight a dragon and make sure you kill it so that your wife and kids won't suffer from hunger."

My father was a wonderful man and his words still haunt me even today. The way his words were so vague; he never even one day bothered himself to explain what he was talking about. We just figured it out for ourselves as we were growing up. When we asked him to elaborate, his response was so simple.

"Grow and be a man of a family. You will understand what was I talking about all along."

Then he continued to puff his traditional tobacco pipe. Jeffrey Mazukulu, the husband of Naddy Mazikulu; our late parents.

You know parents can only give good advice or try to put you on the right path, but the truth is the final forming of a person's character lies in their own hands. The dragon? The dragon was hunger and he meant we must fight it and never allow it to be a permanent scar in our lives; we should fight it with everything we got. Make sure we find a way to defeat it and never allow it to be an everyday visitor in our lives. Always be prepared to fight and defeat it.

After we got retrenched from the oil making factory, Gabriel and I decided to skip the country illegally to South Africa. The hunger was too much and we couldn't watch our wives and kids suffer more and more. We had to act and we came to the point of visiting South Africa. In Zimbabwe they call it, "The mother of peace and love, Jerusalem the land of milk and honey." After we heard a lot of our brothers brainstorming and discussing the ways to skip from Zimbabwe to South Africa, we also became interested and found ourselves joining them with the motives of finding new jobs in order to provide for our families. Finally we arrived in South Africa. For a moment I felt so free like those balloons in birthday parties flying around, all over the place.

But then my taste buds frowned at me the moment I discovered that people of my kind were treated like animals; my taste buds frowned at me the moment I realized it wasn't the same country I thought it was. But still that doesn't stop me from complimenting it further. So we arrived in Cape Town, one of the most beautiful provinces in South Africa. The parts I loved the most about it was that fresh smell of peace surrounding the area, the well-shaped mountain, they call it Table Mountain, not to mention the beautiful ocean full of mature waves, beautiful tall flats, vivid personalities and exquisite smiles of the South African citizens. I fell in love with the thought of visiting South Africa, but it came true because I was finally there. It became true but the aim was not to forget where I came from, my roots. My poor, beautiful Zimbabwean country; it had its struggles but I loved it more than anything in the world. The fact remained that my wife and kids were looking up to me as the hero who was supposed to steal a loaf of bread and feed their hunger with it. That motivated me day in and day out to keep my head up and always find a way to break every obstacle coming my way. To work hard in order to send money to my wife and kids.

The town was so beautiful and mesmerizing, only focus kept me alive. The beautiful colored ladies with their Afrikaans accents, good music, bunny chows, and the beauty of the latest BMWs spinning all over the place drove me insane. The world of entertainment was galore. All those things in our country Zimbabwe, they didn't exist, the freedom of peace wasn't there. Jobs were all over the place here. I became surprised after I learnt that a lot of citizens were complaining about the unemployment rate. I mean, to me jobs were galore: garden jobs, washing cars, packing stocks for Somalians, like it was galore. Honestly speaking, I fell in love with the country. At some point it felt like a vacation, no longer a mission. I wanted to relax and have the time of my life but I couldn't due to reasons. I mean how can you relax while your wife and kids are starving?

Going further with my story. So we arrived there in Cape Town, right? The year was 2012 and we had bags full of clothes but some disappeared on the way because we got chased by the police as we were trying to sneak in. The angry bulldogs with sharp teeth almost served justice by tearing our flesh. The moment we were busy crossing the border from Zimbabwe to South Africa, those border police guards saw us sneaking and chased us with their bulldogs and that's where it became a mess and it didn't end up well for some of my brothers because not all of us lived to tell the tale. Some were captured and sent back to Zimbabwe. Only Gabriel and I and some other folks managed to escape.

Like any other country, South Africa also had its ups and downs, from youth unemployment, corrupt politicians, women Traffickers, drug dealers, rapists with unzipped trousers, illegal strikes; the list is endless. Speaking of illegal strikes, we arrived there with an issue roaming around of police killing miners. The way we heard it gave us goosebumps and left our mouths wide open out of astonishment.

The miners were brutally killed by the police. The story that got every South African questioning themselves about the law, police executing citizens instead of arresting them. *Lonmin Marikana Platinum Mine* located in the north west, it was all over the news and everyone was talking about it. It got me and my brother fearing for our lives; if they can kill their own citizens in that cold blood, where does that leave us? The police were sent there to calm down the angry miners but the way we heard it, the strike was illegal and the angry miners were demanding more salary and better working conditions so the bosses became ignorant to the issue. Somewhere, somehow, the strike began and the angry miners were holding machetes and knobkerries and ready to break anyone's bones for interfering.

The strike was violent and left two cops butchered into pieces by angry miners, and the cops went berserk on them and never bothered themselves to use rubber bullets anymore but to use Alexander Kalashnikov 47's taking a lot of lives. It became a bloodbath; people were shot and killed as if they were some kinds of violent animals. The story left a lot of South Africans with doubts, that maybe it was just an execution.

I mean this is easy. If people are demanding a raise, give them their money. Why hesitate? I'm not a South African citizen but I sympathize with them on this one. Each and every person has the right to be treated fairly and with respect. The strike left 34 miners dead and 78 others injured. It was bloodshed and those Alexander Kalashnikovs were blazing on the flesh of innocent miners who just wanted to be treated fairly. Police claimed that the miners were armed and it was some kind of self-defense. An extreme violence coming from the members of law enforcement. How tragic.

We arrived and survived because the motive was not to cause trouble but to find some punching gloves in order to fight the hunger in our lives. We left Zimbabwe due to hunger and in South Africa it was better. As foreigners we had to live under the bridges, because the rooms to rent were not there and we didn't have enough money to afford a rental room. Take any job as long as you can send money home to your family, *that* was the goal. We were living with hobos and drug addicts under those bridges and they were stealing from us so bad, but we couldn't confront them because we were not original citizens of the country. That means we had to keep quiet even when they were stepping on our toes. For peace, only silence was relevant. Imagine working so hard for money with the aim to send it to your family, then someone just comes out of nowhere and steals it. Some of the months I had to lie to my wife and come up with stories of why I couldn't send money to her because they were eating the rewards of my labour for free. It was impossible to open a bank account because we were foreigners, not original citizens of the country.

The salary of the multiple jobs I was doing was fair. Washing cars, gardening, and brick collection on construction sites, the pay was to be sent home. Sometimes we had to starve ourselves for our families. Then I managed to run a race then fell into the right hands. The job was permanent and we were gardeners in Mrs. Forbes home. An old colored woman, I think she was between 45 and 50 years old, somewhere there. She was a very wealthy woman in a 15-room double story house and it had a single room separate. Her children were overseas and she became generous to us as her gardeners and offered us the single room to stay rent-free. She had a huge love for roses and her yard was full of them. We were hired to plant more and nurture them. She became a hero to us, because there in the streets, it was not promising anymore; the xenophobic attacks were starting to dominate. Our brothers were dying.

The South Africans were tired of us as foreigners in their country. The human trafficking scandal was roaming all over the news that a Nigerian man named Okonkwo Abhudabhi was found with a 17 year old teenage girl and got arrested in the airport trying to skip the country with her. The teenager was reported missing for years. He made bail after 1 week, but he never lived to tell a tale. He was somehow captured by the teenager's father and butchered, then fed to the sharks. The crime cases were dominating almost every day. Another case was reported that a Zimbabwean man was dealing drugs in the streets of Cape Town and he sold a pack of *blue magic* drug to a teenager that caused an instant death to the boy. The colored citizens went berserk and decided to take the law in their own hands.

Drug dealing and human trafficking rate was high and foreign names dominated the police dockets, one potato makes the other rotten. Some of us suffered the repercussions of other people actions. The teenage boy who was killed by the pack of *blue magic* drugs, he was not just a teenage boy from neighborhood families. He was Tony Maguire's little brother, a well-known ex-convict and a gang leader in prison and even outside of the prison. He ruled the streets of Cape Town. After the death of his little brother by the hands of foreigners, he organized a gang and they only had one goal: to hunt and kill foreigners. Honestly speaking, it was a mess. Our brothers were shot, beaten and even butchered by Maguire and his goons.

I had to watch my brother praying multiple times a day. Xenophobic attacks were all over the place and our safety was in Mrs. Forbes' single room. The question was, for how long? Some were burnt and some were butchered. He was angry and he just wanted to spill blood. Whether you came looking for job, as a painter or an engineer, he didn't care. Shops were burnt down and some were thrown into the cages for bulldogs to feed on them.

One night my brother and I decided to take our chances and visit the Mukuru branch in order to send money home. We managed to send it and my wife Loraine was so happy. We were also planning to work for only one month then disappear because the attacks were getting out of hand. Our brothers were slaves to death and our brothers were also meat to the hungry dogs. Tony Maguire was tired of police not doing their jobs and the corruption they were doing. The man who sold those drugs to his little brother managed to bribe one of the officials, and after he was released he disappeared, leaving us to face the repercussions of his actions.

It was around 8pm at night. Gabriel and I were discussing the ways to escape. Because it was a bloodbath almost every day, they were in a group of seven. With them they had guns, machetes, daggers and golf sticks. Walking toward us and suddenly they stopped, then Tony appeared out of nowhere. Tall in height, in his body he had tattoos including on his face, one on the right cheek and one on the forehead. A real badass, the spirit of death was heating up my chest and in my nose was a scent of blood but I wasn't bleeding, I knew it was my last night. Holding a piece of cigarette burning his lungs out and also holding a golf stick. His goons slowly surrounding us, and whistling with violent weapons in their hands.

"Please we did not come to your country to cause trouble!!" I confessed. Their mocking laughs were on another level.

"Don't kill us, we only came here to work and provide for our families!!" I confessed for the second time.

One of the goons pulled out a pistol. The reflection of its nose was so clear because of the bright light of the moon.

"Have mercy on us!!"

As I was confessing, I heard something heavy hitting the back of my skull, then I saw a river of blood coming out in a violent way. I fell near Tony and he was there still smoking while his other goons where still wiping their daggers.

"Please, Tony, don't kill us."

My brother trying his luck, as I was still on the ground dealing with the pain and slowly getting up. Fear of death.

"Will that bring my brother back to life?"

His anger was on another level. As I was trying to come up with an answer, he threw that piece of cigarette he was smoking and pulled a pistol, aimed, then pulled the trigger more than once. I just heard the angry cough of his gun. Then I saw Gabriel slowly falling and his shirt was covered in blood, his chest was full of river, a river of blood. I saw him coughing blood out of his mouth. I ran to him ignoring the pain in the back of my skull. I grabbed him and tried to calm him down. Then I saw tears coming out of his eyes slowly. Then I saw him breathing his last breath and his eyes slowly closing themselves. He killed my little brother with six bullets, three on his head and three on his chest. I felt the soft water coming out of my eyes, then I squeezed his hand so hard and cried in silence. I heard something hot entering from that fresh wound in the back of my head and blowing my brains inside my head in a huge speed of fire. Then I lost control of my body, slowly fell on top of my little brother's corpse. Then I saw Tony wiping his gun and his goon were praising him.

"Nice shot, Boss!!"

I felt the oxygen slowly leaving my body and my eyes were slowly closing themselves and I couldn't control it. We only came to work not to cause trouble but we ended up dead in the streets of Cape Town. We paid a meal we didn't eat with our lives.

Zshaboombi: The Plight of Contrition

By Ivan S Mooh Mooh

A story from Cameroon

My darling Elizabeth,

The heavens are weeping here; their cries have not ceased for the past three nights. The raindrops crashing down violently on the silver zinc roofs of all the inhabitants of Atembe. Listening to the harsh symphony being composed by this never-ending rainstorm, reminds me of that old cottage in Edinburgh, the one almost a decade ago where we shared our first kiss.

I wish before God and all the archangels of Saint Peters Court that you were here now by my side as I write you this letter. I know beyond a shadow of a doubt, if you were here with me tonight, I could forget this rain.

No one thought to enlighten me on the climate I would face in Africa (I reckon father sent me here purposefully ignorant to give my holiday an added spice.) Nonetheless, it was quite a daunting task to get properly acclimated upon arrival in Zshaboombi.

I reckon mainly due to the vastness of the British Empire, there is not enough time in the world to indoctrinate you on all her colonies. So, for you my darling Elizabeth, I shall just try to speak of Zshaboombi.

Zshaboombi is one of the five colonies of her majesty's empire in West Africa: an aggregation that used to consist of The Gold Coast, Sierra Leone, Nigeria, and the Gambia. Zshaboombi borders are adjacent to Nigeria in the East, and Liberia to the West. It's a country with quite a fascinating history.

Originally a German colony after the great partition of Africa during the Berlin Conference of 1884 by Otto Von Bismarck, it was later split in half by our government and the French after both Great Wars (during which Germany had to relinquish all her colonies).

We the English govern the country's Western territories (my uncle Benjamin being one of the many political Viceroys who work as administrators for her majesty's government in the region), and the French govern the Eastern region of Zshaboombi. Thus has been the arrangement since the end of the Second Great War in 1945.

During my fourth week in Zshaboombi, my uncle Benjamin reckoned it would be a good idea for me to "explore the glory which we the English have built in the West of Zshaboombi." So indeed, I was sent off exploring. He gave me some money and his main houseboy, Mbonifor, was my guide.

Mbonifor resembled me in age, or so I thought. I remember asking him how old he was and being shocked that he was only four years my junior. Mbonifor was a large man, with skin dark as dawn, his mass lean and rippling with muscles. It was ludicrous to me that an individual this large and strong could only be eighteen.

After my uncle gave his instructions, Mbonifor obediently carried them out. Thus, I followed him out of the villa, and into the great capital city of Western Zshaboombi: Atembe.

The city of Atembe is broken up into three districts: The Western District, The Eastern District, and The Southern District.

The Western District is home mostly to fellow Englishmen (it's also where Uncle Benjamin's government villa, the place where I'm writing this letter, resides). All English Magistrates and Viceroy's rule the entire of Western Zshaboombi from this part of Atembe; rarely do they ever leave the West.

The Eastern District houses all the ministers and Viceroys of the French government. From this part of Atembe, France commands all matters in the East of Zshaboombi. Finally, there's the place of Mbonifors origin: The Southern District.

I imagine when you've heard talk of Africa, tales have been spun regarding naked savages carrying out Tarzan-like activities with spears, running amok in the wild jungle covered in feces, completely incapable of speaking English or acting civilized. This perversion of Africa couldn't be further from the truth: especially here in Zshaboombi.

Elizabeth, there is a marketplace in the Southern District; a market like no other. Zshaboosians dressed in all kinds of ways walk that market, some in English suits, others in traditional African Kabas; buying and selling, haggling and bartering. It was madness, yet, I suppose in a way, it was organized madness.

Zshaboosians would shout and get angry with one another over the cost of cassava, but eventually, both parties would see reason. Small boys and other children ran around the market, chasing one another with sticks. Live hens and cocks of numerous colours in cages crowed. Fenced in pigs squealed. The red and brown dust from the market seemed to be moving, flying about from the red peppers left in the open, to the cut meats blazed over a fire by vendors throughout.

I reckon prior to arriving on this holiday in Zshaboombi, I too had fallen victim to the pejorative fiction peddled in regard to this continent (this is to say that Joseph Conrad's *Heart of Darkness* might be the greatest lie ever told during the 19th Century).

I would return to the villa later that evening and dine with Uncle Benjamin, giving him an account of my day.

After supper was concluded and Mbonifor cleared the table, my uncle and I went out into the rose garden, smoking Dutch cigars and drinking brandy. We touched on numerous topics as we drank: politics, the economy, philosophy, but most importantly, I remember he kept shifting the conversation towards what plans I had for my life after graduation from Oxford next year.

I lied to him, telling him I did not know, knowing full well precisely what I've always wanted to do, just always being too afraid to tell both my father and uncle. I knew that both these men I shared direct lineage with were individuals with the lust for greatness: regretfully a character trait I have always lacked.

I kept my uncle ignorant of all this as we smoked, drank, and talked, allowing him to believe my future was still unplanned. That's when he told me my father's reason for sending me to Zshaboombi for this holiday.

"Elliot, soon it shall come time for you to take your place in the world. My brother believes that place for you is here in Zshaboombi. He intends for you to become a Viceroy in the near future and, someday soon, Prime Minister. That is the opportunity behind this holiday, to introduce you to your new life. Following this weekend, Zshaboombi celebrates twenty-three years of joint rule by her majesty's government and the French. A gala will be thrown here, and it is here you shall be introduced to the politicians and magistrates who are essential to your destiny. Elliot, I need not remind you that you are a Pemberton; a name like that holds great privilege, and thus with it, great duty. The time is soon coming when you will have to live up to that name. Do us proud, nephew!"

After our talk, my uncle bid me goodnight. I remember when I retired to my chamber that evening, I was overcome by one distinct emotion: sadness.

Thus, the fifth week of my stay in Zshaboombi came, and my father's and uncle's plans for my destiny continued to be set in motion. Mbonifor did as he had been instructed by my uncle, continuing to give me tours of Atembe. Mbonifor never spoke much; he was a man of few emotions and even fewer words.

We toured the Western District, which I disliked profusely. The entire Western District is a low-cost replica of England, the streets matching the tar and cobbled roads of London, and the people there emanating the same ambiance of pompous self-righteousness that is found everywhere back home.

It was the Eastern District that most surprised me. It happened towards the end of my fifth week in Atembe. Mbonifor and I were at a market in the Eastern District shopping for bangers because there were none left at the villa. As we were looking for the sausages, we saw a tall, burly, Frenchman, with a fine, coiled moustache crossing the market road, and as he crossed, he purposefully sent his shoulder flying into the chest of a Zshaboosian crossing the street with him.

The Zshaboosian screamed out in great pain and fell to the ground in agony, his cry gained the attention of all who were present in the market.

The tall Frenchman clearly seemed annoyed that the Zshaboosian had cried out in pain. As though to say, "here's something to really cry about," he sent his black boot crashing down on the Zshaboosian's face, then he repeated the gesture over and over again.

Everyone in the market cheered as he did. A rupture of enabling chants rang out in French throughout the whole market. All the

French people were chanting something in unison as the tall Frenchman with the peculiar moustache kept stomping on the visage of the helpless Zshaboosian on the ground.

After what seemed like an eternity, the tall Frenchman stopped stomping and kicking the Zshaboosian in his face. His black boot was by then completely covered in blood.

The Frenchman gargled his saliva and spit very purposefully on the body of the bloody Zshaboosian lying unconscious on the ground, then he wiped his boot on the poor man's clothes and walked onward until he was out of sight. No one bothered to aid the Zshaboosian lying unconscious on the ground. The French people just walked over him, as though he didn't exist.

When Mbonifor and I headed back to the villa that day with the bangers, I asked him why that Frenchman had committed such a despicable act of random violence.

At first Mbonifor said nothing, but then eventually he spoke. "Europeans are never wrong in this country. All their actions are just, no matter the situation. Sir, you will one day soon come to learn that though Zshaboosians are no longer slaves, that does not mean we are free."

Then I asked him what it was that the crowd was chanting in unison back at the market, he responded, "They were saying *'tuez le singe.'* It is French. It means kill the monkey."

Since I disliked the Western District, and feared the Eastern, I spent most of my time in the Southern District.

At first, the inhabitants of the Southern District were formal around me, naturally showing their distrust, but after a few days of us playing football (and my side constantly getting humiliated by a ludicrous goal margin), an unspoken friendliness grew to exist between me and the local people.

The small children there, bilingual from birth, even went out of their way to teach me some rudimentary French, (despite their age, their English was far better than mine, and their mastery of the French language would have turned even De Gaulle green with envy).

It was during this time, towards the final days of my fifth week in Zshaboombi, when I became aware of the fact that not only was Mbonifor married, but that he was also a father.

My uncle had given Mbonifor the day off, so when I awoke that morning and asked around for him, no one knew where to find him. Eventually I asked my uncle and he told me, then he gave me Mbonifor's address in the Southern District, to which I quickly departed.

Upon arrival at the address, I was greeted by a sweet, dark little girl, who looked no older than two. Her teeth were still forming. The only ones present at the time where her front two. When she smiled up at me, I couldn't help but smile back. She was followed by her mother: a tall, brown woman, with ethnic hair. She curtsied to me as they did during the days of old England. I remember becoming flush with embarrassment, quickly telling her she didn't have to.

Then, Mbonifor walked into the room. His eyes fresh with the rings of sleep around them. Instantly, he seemed to wake up at seeing me there in his home.

A tense silence filled the room we were all in. Both Mbonifor and his wife casted a strange look at me. It was at that moment that his daughter escaped from the grasp of her mother and ran to me, crashing directly into my knee. The little girl started to cry. I carried her into my arms and started consoling her, rocking her back and forth. Mbonifor saw his daughter in my arms and his eyes instantly filled with fear and horror. I saw this and I immediately put her down.

Almost seconds later, his daughter stopped crying and started to play with my knee, fascinated by it somehow. This caused Mbonifor's wife and I to laugh.

His wife invited me to join them for breakfast. I looked over at Mbonifor, almost asking for permission. He nodded his head slightly at me, at which I accepted his wife's invitation. We had a Zshaboosian breakfast: eggs and *Ayongo* bread (wheat bread that has been sweetened). It was delicious, and for the first time since I'd known him, I saw Mbonifor smile.

After breakfast was done, he and I cleared the table and went out for a stroll. As we walked, he spoke to me about his wife, Akwanni, and his daughter, Josephine. I tried to impress Mbonifor with some of the newly learned French I had been taught by the Zshaboosian children of the Southern District. He only laughed at my feeble attempts to grasp the difference between *chat* and *chien.* It had taken me five weeks, but for the first time in a very long time, I had chosen a friend that I wanted.

At last, the final day of the fifth week came, a Sunday, the biblical day of rest. It also happened to be the day Uncle Benjamin was throwing his gala celebrating the duopoly of governance in Zshaboombi.

It was an all-white affair, quite literally.

I walked around the room with Uncle Benjamin in my perfectly tailored white tux, greeting and conversing with all the guests.

I had talks with the governor of Western Zshaboombi, a certain Lord Winston Castlestark, and finally, my worst nightmare, the governor of Eastern Zshaboombi, Monsieur Hugo Bastian Deschamps, the tall, burly Frenchman with the moustache from the incident at the French market a week prior.

The colour left my face, and fright must have filled my eyes, because as we shook hands, Governor Deschamps asked in very heavily accented English if I was alright.

I lied and said I was fine, shaking his hand back with strength I never knew I had. He beamed a genuine smile at my uncle, showing off his perfect teeth. He told my uncle I had the grip of a bear, to which my uncle laughed, and patted me approvingly on the back.

Both men then broke out into a rapid conversation of French (a language I never knew Uncle Benjamin spoke fluently till then). I tried to excuse myself from the conversation, but Uncle Benjamin wouldn't allow it. So, I just stood there, looking terribly awkward, watching these two powerful men exchange words.

It was very clear from the onset of the conversation that Governor Deschamps held more power in Zshaboombi than my uncle, because as they conversed, I noticed my uncle addressed him solely in the formal French pronoun of *Vous* and Governor Deschamps addressed him in the French informal of *Tu*.

The conversation both men were having must have suddenly somehow switched to the topic of firearms, because a moment later, Governor Deschamps removed a small pistol from his waistcoat. He gave it to my uncle to examine, who in turn marvelled at the weapon. He eventually passed it to me.

Governor Deschamps eyes bored into me, examining me as I held his weapon. Then, a few moments later, he reached out for his pistol, which I returned, and then he walked away from the both of us. Soon after, the bell rang for evening supper.

As dinner was served, and as we all ate, we discussed philosophy. Uncle Benjamin gave the two heads of the table to both the Governors of Eastern and Western Zshaboombi. They dictated which philosophers were appropriate to discuss and which weren't.

Montesquieu was loved that night, while Robespierre was hated. Malthus was an enlightened prophet, and Hobbs a raving lunatic. Dialogue over Africa and freedom from the colonial system was the topic of conversation when dessert arrived. Dessert was a black frosted, red devil cake.

When Mbonifor went to place Governor Deschamps cake in front of him, the Governor purposefully moved his elbow in an upward manner, causing the cake that was to be placed directly in front of him, to be squashed on the elbow area of his white tux, the black frosting leaving a very noticeable stain.

Clearly everyone at the table had seen Governor Deschamps commit this act on purpose, but we all said nothing. Instead, Uncle Benjamin scolded Mbonifor for being careless.

The table went silent as we all waited for what Governor

Deschamps would say. A pin drop could have been heard during our wait.

Governor Deschamps eyes went from his caked elbow, to Mbonifor. Then he said something very slowly in French involving a monkey, because I heard those all too familiar words: *le singe.*

After the governor spoke, Mbonifor bowed his head and apologized. Then he raised his head and courteously excused himself, I assumed to get a cloth or napkin for Governor Deschamps soiled tux.

As Mbonifor walked away, conversation returned to the table, people drank champagne again and tasted sweet things, but I knew something was awry. I could see it in Governor Deschamps eyes: this wasn't over for him. He shouted for Mbonifor to stop walking away and turn around.

Immediately, all conversation at the table ceased again.

Mbonifor complied to Governor Deschamps order, turning around exactly where he had stopped.

Governor Deschamps rose from the head of the dinner table and began to walk over to Mbonifor. He then pulled out the silver pistol from his waistcoat and pointed it at Mbonifor.

It was then that Governor Deschamps pulled the trigger twice.

The two loudest explosions I will ever hear in my life filled the dining room. After which Mbonifor's lifeless body fell loudly to the floor.

Blood started to leak out from the two holes in Mbonifor's chest and pool onto the white tiles.

Governor Deschamps returned to his seat at the head of the table. When finally seated again, he turned to my uncle and said in English, "My apologies, Benjamin. Your monkey soiled my suit, I lost my temper."

My uncle shook his head sympathetically and then said in response, "All is well, sir. The fault was his anyway. Besides, my monkey can be replaced, your suit cannot." The dinner table erupted with great bouts of laughter at my uncle's joke, especially Governor Deschamps, who even gave Uncle Benjamin an approving pat on the back.

I was sick to my stomach, quite literally. I excused myself from the dinner table and ran out into the rose garden to vomit. I never returned to finish dessert.

As I write this to you now, Elizabeth, it has been three days since Mbonifor was murdered. My uncle had his body delivered for burial to his family. I wasn't there to see its arrival, but I can only imagine the ripple effects of pain and grief Governor Deschamps' cruelty has brought to Akwanni and Josephine. A wife is without a husband, a daughter without her father, a mother without a son, and I am without my friend.

The rains started the day following Mbonifor's funeral, and they haven't stopped since. I don't want them to ever stop, for the whole world should mourn along with me for the loss of my friend.

I am a weak man, Elizabeth. I have been all my life. I have never had the strength to stand for anything, besides the love we share for one another. The love I have for you is the one constant in this world which nothing can change, which no man can ever take from me.

My love, you are my home.

I am Odysseus lost at sea, and you are Penelope, faithfully awaiting my return by the isles of Ithaca.

You are my harbour after a raging storm, and I am coming home to you now. I've been away for far too long.

The Irish philosopher Sir Edmund Burke once wrote, "The only thing necessary for the triumph of evil is for good men to do nothing."

I am complicit in the murder of my friend. Though I did not pull the trigger, I may as well have by never saying or doing anything to prevent it. Truly, may God have mercy on all our souls, and may Mbonifor finally find peace in the bosom of the lord, resting peacefully for all eternity in the presence of Saint Peter.

Forever and always, with all my love,

Elliot Aloysius Pemberton.

ABOUT THE AUTHORS

Biographies for the top 3 winners are given below.

Radha Zutshi Opubor, author of *The Travelling Man*, is a 17-year-old Indian-Nigerian girl living in London. Her work has previously appeared in *Omenana*, the *Kalahari Review*, and the Afrofuturism Issue of *Chicago Literati*. In February of 2021, her short story 'The Flood' (*Omenana* 8/20) was selected for the 2020 *Locus* Recommended Reading List.

Favour Modekwe, author of *Ifechukwu*, is from Nigeria. She is a graduate of zoology currently a PG.D student of education. She loves nature and enjoys reading, writing and travelling.

Ifeyinwa Judith Ogwo, author of *The Magic Claypot*, is a native of Nkitaku village, Agulu in Anaocha local government area, Anambra State, Nigeria. She has three brothers and one sister. She had her Primary, Secondary and University education in Benin-City, Edo State, Nigeria.